Daniel's Esperanza

Veronica Randolph Batterson

ISBN: 1500398926
ISBN 13: 9781500398927

AUTHOR'S NOTE

In 1971, Congress passed the *Wild Free-Roaming Horse and Burro Act* to protect the wild mustang. The act required that mustangs be protected as "living symbols of the historic and pioneer spirit of the west". This act stands today, yet these beautiful animals continue to be threatened, often due to the number of herds grazing on the same public land that cattle ranchers use via lease rights given to them by the Bureau of Land Management. Too often this results in roundups or "gatherings", which the BLM insists is necessary to control herd populations and prevents over foraging of the land, with those horses in captivity being made available for public adoptions. Wild horse advocates call the roundups cruel due to the methods used and say the holding areas don't provide sufficient space and shade in the sweltering heat of summer to hold the horses.

When this book was written, horse slaughter had once again been legalized in this country. It was written into the storyline as such. Since publication, the atrocity has been banned, at least temporarily, in the United States yet third parties have found a way to sell horses (oftentimes from roundups) to kill buyers who will sell and ship to slaughterhouses in Canada and Mexico. Horse slaughter is cruel and inhumane, and until it is permanently made illegal, the threats continue.

There are many wild horse advocates in the United States who work tirelessly to save the American Mustang. They have dogged determination and energy. If those reading this are interested in volunteering and/or supporting the cause, some of the well known organizations include The Cloud Foundation, American Wild Horse Preservation Campaign, Salt River Wild Horses, Corolla Wild Horse Fund, Black Hills Wild Horse Sanctuary and Saving America's Mustangs.

Finally, this book is a work of fiction and all characters are fictional. The Native American storyline and descriptions are not representative of the Navajo Nation.

ACKNOWLEDGMENTS

Three years ago, research for this book took me on an enlightening journey to New Mexico. Driving north from Santa Fe, my husband and I stopped in Tierra Amarilla, a small town off US Highway 84, near Chama. The route took us through Georgia O'Keeffe country and some of the most scenic and unique views this area has to offer. It was in this setting that we found Monero Mustangs Sanctuary. Owned and operated by Sandi Claypool, it was a haven dedicated to the preservation of the American Mustang.

Recently, Monero Mustangs Sanctuary was forced to move the wild horses off the land it had occupied. Sandi never stopped working, relocating the horses to a temporary place, then finding forever homes for these beautiful animals.

Thank you, Sandi Claypool, for being a wild horse advocate and for giving a voice to these magnificent creatures. Seeing you work in the setting you loved allowed me to create this story.

As always, I give sincere thanks to my family. Forever my proofreaders, listeners and moral supporters, their patience and belief in me encourage my creative treks to continue along these fictional journeys. Much love and appreciation to all.

Daniel's Esperanza

CHAPTER ONE

He breathed deeply and let the cold air fill his lungs. The windows were rolled down on the old pickup truck and it rejuvenated him. He'd endured a cold winter in northern New Mexico and Mother Nature didn't seem too eager to let spring take over. The wind hit Daniel in the face and made him see things for what they were. He knew the dream he'd had couldn't hurt him. But it was his recurring nightmare. All of it based on reality that Daniel had lived not too long ago, but escaped with help. His eyes watered, from the memories and the cold air, and he wiped the wetness on the back of his sleeve, driving on.

Daniel drove down the dirt road and heard only the hum of the engine and the sound of tires crunching over thawing ice puddles and gravel. He was an interruption to the peaceful quiet of night but didn't care. Daniel knew exactly where he was going and it helped him clear his head. It was the same place he drove to every time he felt troubled about something.

The headlights found the side road he was searching for and he turned left. He didn't brake soon enough and the sudden change in speed caused the back tires to skid. But he straightened the truck sharply and found the road again. Daniel knew within a couple of weeks all of the snow and ice would turn to a thawed mess. The side road might not even be accessible until after the thaws. Last spring, he'd walked up the road, driving as far as he could and then parked

1

just before the flooded area. It had taken longer to walk the mesa but he felt better for it. It was too cold and slippery to do that now.

The truck inched along. The road was narrow and on an incline so Daniel maneuvered carefully, trying not to lose control and hit any ice. He kept his eyes on the road and was surprised when something small darted across in front of him. "I must not be the only one having trouble sleeping," he mumbled, driving along, hoping he didn't encounter whatever had stirred that critter from its slumber.

He finally reached his destination. Slowing the truck to a stop, Daniel grabbed his flashlight and got out of the vehicle. Just a short distance from the road stood the ruins of an ancient kiva. The Anasazi used kivas for spiritual rituals and this one had been abandoned long ago. Even though no longer in use, Daniel knew better than to do anything that might damage it further. It was considered sacred and he respected the customs of the people he had gotten to know over the last three years.

The kiva was located on the ten thousand acres he now called home, but was close to the Indian reservation nearby. Once when sitting up here meditating his first summer, he felt a presence behind him. He had turned quickly but saw nothing. Thinking it was the late afternoon shadows playing tricks on him, he turned around only to hear a rustling sound to his right. Looking, he didn't see anything. Then he heard the laugh and turned to see a boy standing in front of him.

Daniel jumped up at the sight, losing his balance and falling backward. That had made the boy laugh even harder. The intruder was shorter than Daniel and his skin was dark. He wore clothing that looked too large for him, probably hand-me-downs, and Daniel guessed the kid was from the reservation. He also noticed the boy walked with a limp.

"You shouldn't sneak up on people," Daniel had said.

"You have yellow hair," the boy replied, laughing, then turned around and ran.

It wasn't long after the encounter that Daniel started seeing the boy around more. He'd show up while Daniel was working with the horses or out in the hay fields. He was always watching Daniel but seemed afraid or too shy to approach him. There was always a smile on his face and his animated eyes held mischief. It took a long time for Daniel to coax a name from him but eventually the boy blurted, "You can call me Joe".

"Nice to meet you, 'You can call me Joe'," Daniel said, smiling.

That had made the boy laugh into the wind. From that point on, Joe was at Daniel's side whenever he was able. Curious and energetic, he was always asking questions and doing things to help. Joe took particular interest in Bob, the rescued mixed-breed dog that lived with Daniel. It was easy to like Bob, but Joe seemed fascinated with the animal, as if he'd never been around a dog before. Daniel knew otherwise, as dogs were allowed to roam all over the reservation.

The sound of scratching brought Daniel back to the present. He held up the flashlight, straining his eyes to see what might be in its cast of light. He immediately thought of Joe, but knew he wouldn't have been around at this time of the night. Plus, it was too cold for any of those kids to be out. It was too cold for him, too, he thought, shivering. He wasn't sure if it was the cold or if the unknown sound caused the goose bumps that were creeping down his arms. Probably nothing, he reasoned as he lowered the light.

Most of his visits to this special place were during the daylight hours, but he had made the trip in the middle of the night before. He'd had the nightmare and felt the need to come here. It probably wasn't the wisest choice he'd ever made, coming up here after dark. There were wild animals roaming the ranch but the need for air and a clear head were greater than the fear of wildlife encounters.

It was always the same. In his dream, he was running from the devil. But the devil kept morphing into the bastard Daniel had grown up fearing. His father's face grew closer in the dream as Daniel struggled to run away from it. He'd spent the first fifteen years of his life dodging fists his father threw in alcoholic rages and mean abusiveness. Daniel had endured broken ribs, split lips, blackened eyes, belt whelps and emergency surgery from a fall down the stairs. The devil had pushed him. Of course, the story told to the hospital staff was he'd fallen.

His mother hadn't been any better. Mental illness controlled her life and she refused treatment for it. Fury consumed her most days, while fantasy mingled with reality. Reality slipped farther away each day. She usually thought Daniel had deserved whatever punch her husband doled out, as she worshipped the ground the man walked on. But the old man was known to abuse her as well. She died three years ago from an overdose of sleeping pills. Daniel couldn't muster enough sympathy to shed a tear.

He was fifteen years old when his mother died. The funeral had been held in the morning and very few people attended. His family didn't have many friends and the handful of people who gave their respects probably did so out of guilt and concern for him. They knew what he'd endured and had done nothing about it. The neighbors could hear the shouting and cursing from both his parents, but turned deaf ears to it. Sounds of shattered glass and the recurring slaps rang out in the silence of the night but help never came. People pretended his life was as good as theirs. It was easier and less messy that way. When they would see his bloody nose or black eye, they'd look the other way, pretending they hadn't. He grew to resent it.

After the funeral, Daniel remembered returning home to an empty house. His father had gone to the nearest bar. Daniel was thankful he was an only child because he figured he could handle his father's meanness. He didn't think he could have put up with a brother or sister getting the same treatment. It would have driven him to do something that might have landed him in prison.

He had grown tall and strong. It would take very little to fight back as his father's form was degenerating from alcoholic consumption, his muscles wasting away. One punch from Daniel would have sent his old man across the room, but fighting was something he found distasteful. He refused the temptation, promising himself that he wouldn't follow that path. So he took everything that was thrown at him. But he thought it probably would've been different if there had been a sibling to protect.

And something about that day was different. He was tired. Tired of walking on eggshells, worrying if he coughed a certain way that it

4

would send his father into a blind rage. He was tired of being afraid and tired of feeling worthless. He was tired of being yelled at and knocked around. And he was tired of never getting a kind word or feeling the love you're supposed to get from a parent.

His eyes had burned from the tears that fell. He wasn't sad for the loss of his mother. He was sad because of life. It had given him a raw deal and he found nothing he wished to live for. Daniel remembered the pets he'd tried to have over the years. There had been a puppy here or there when he was young. The joy those squirming little bodies gave his heart were the happiest times he could remember. But they always seemed to disappear. He'd get up for school or come home in the afternoon, and his mother would make some excuse or another for their absence. When he was little, he never questioned why. It just made him sad and he'd cry himself to sleep over it at night, never stopping until his father would come into his room, slapping and punching him until he stopped crying.

The last dog he'd ever had died due to a kick his father gave him in the side. The puppy was playing with a ball and got in his father's way. Daniel watched the devil kick the pup so hard that the little body slammed against the far wall and slumped to the floor. It didn't move. The devil turned to Daniel and laughed, saying, "Next time he'll know better."

There was no next time. Daniel buried the dog in the back yard. It occurred to him then that his father was the reason he'd never kept a pet. He didn't wish to know what kind of suffering the devil put the poor animals through, but he swore he'd never have another one. At least not while his father could harm it.

He heard the sound of his father's car in the driveway. Daniel knew what would come and he didn't think he could take anymore of it. He'd had enough and he needed to find a way to get out. He had a little bit of money saved, from part time jobs he had worked. It was money he had to hide from his father, lying that he didn't have any so it wouldn't be spent on alcohol. Maybe the money could buy him a bus ticket somewhere. Then he'd find a job doing something. It didn't matter. Anything was better than the hell he'd been living in.

"Danny!" the devil yelled, stumbling through the door.

When he gave no answer, the devil yelled again, this time a little louder.

"When I call your name, you answer me, you hear?" his father spat, his shirttail pulled from his pants and his hair sticking up. His eyes were glazed and Daniel knew he was drunk. Daniel felt disgust for the man standing in front of him and his insides burned with hatred for the person he had the misfortune of knowing as his father.

"That's how you want to play it? All right then. No boy of mine is going to treat me with disrespect," the devil spat, reaching to unbuckle the belt fastened at his waist. "Bend over that couch so I can get you good."

"No. Not anymore," Daniel said quietly.

"You shut your goddamn mouth, you worthless piece of crap. Get over here now!" he screamed.

Daniel stood his ground. The devil's eyes glowed with meanness. If he could wish for anything at the moment, it would've been for the old man to be struck dead right then and there.

"Boy, I'm warnin' you. You better do as I say, or else," the devil hissed.

"Or else what? Get a beating if I come over there or get one if I don't. Why should I make it easy for you?" Daniel asked. He didn't know where the words were coming from but it felt good to say them.

"Why, you, son of a bitch! Boy, I'll teach you a lesson you'll never forget," the old man spewed, lunging for Daniel, but missing and falling over the coffee table with a thud and landing on the floor.

Daniel looked at the pile of flesh and bones on the floor. The pile didn't make an effort to move after the fall and Daniel assumed the devil had passed out. Seconds passed and there was a knock on the front door.

He made his way around his father's form to the door and opened it. Standing there was an old friend of his mother's, a man that Daniel only knew as 'Charley'. Charley had always been referenced when his mother was fighting with his father. Whatever the argument, Charley was the savior his mother passed up to marry the devil. That was thrown in his old man's face time and again, yet his sick mother couldn't get enough of the man she did marry. It was something Daniel would never understand. If Charley was so great, why did she stay with, or better yet, marry an abusive man?

"Danny, is everything okay?" Charley asked.

"Don't call me Danny. My name's Daniel," he replied. The devil always called him 'Danny' or 'boy', whichever suited his mood.

"I'm sorry. Daniel, then. Is everything okay?" Charley repeated.

"What do you think?" Daniel asked as a response. He stepped aside to let the man enter and both looked at the passed out man on the floor.

"He's drunk, I guess," Charley said.

"Yes, that's his specialty," Daniel said.

"Look, Daniel. We don't have a lot of time, so listen to me carefully. I have a friend who's willing to help you. I should've done this a long time ago," he said, pulling something from his shirt pocket.

"I bought a bus ticket for you. To New Mexico. You'll have a place to stay and work, even get your diploma. But the best part is you won't be taking this anymore," Charley said, nodding his head toward the lump on the ground.

"Why would you do this for me?" Daniel asked. His head was spinning. He had never been to New Mexico and knew very little about it.

"Because I'm tired of being a coward and it's the right thing to do," he replied, "no one should have to live like this."

"I guess that doesn't really answer my question," Daniel said.

"I'm the reason your mother married that monster, plain and simple. She was a spiteful woman, God rest her soul. She got angry with me because I didn't propose marriage when she thought I should've," Charley explained, "so she met your father at a bar and eloped with him that very night. She was too proud to admit she'd made a mistake."

"Even at the expense of her own son," Daniel mumbled, looking at the ticket the man held.

"Well, I can't even fathom someone cold enough to allow such things to happen to a child, but I know I won't let it happen anymore. That's why I'm here. Take this," Charley said, handing the bus ticket to him.

"Won't he come looking for me?" Daniel asked, pointing at the devil.

"Maybe, maybe not. In all likelihood, he won't. Oh, he'll be mad enough at first, but I'll do everything in my power to keep your whereabouts a secret," said Charley.

"But what if he contacts the police? Won't they try to find me and bring me back? I couldn't take that," Daniel said.

"Your father wouldn't chance the police finding out about the life of horrors he's put you through if he involves them. So, I don't think he will," Charley said, extending the ticket to him again.

Daniel took the ticket from Charley. It was his way out and he was going to take it. He didn't know what kind of life to expect but he knew with all of his heart it would be better than what he'd been dealt. His father snored loudly.

"Hurry, get moving. Go pack some clothes and I'll wait here. I don't want him to wake up before we go," Charley said.

"We?" Daniel asked.

"I'm driving you to the bus station, and seeing firsthand that you get on that bus. I have a little money to help you, it's not much, but I have some. Now, hurry," the man said urgently.

Daniel packed his few belongings, the little bit of money he'd saved and left the only home he'd ever known. He took the money Charley handed him before boarding the bus.

"I'll pay you back someday," Daniel told the man.

"The only payback I need is to know you've found a happy life," Charley replied.

Daniel nodded and asked suddenly, "Do you think I might have a dog at this new place?"

"Oh, I don't think that'll be a problem. As a matter of fact, you'll find more than just dogs in your new life," Charley smiled, patting him on the back. "Now, go. I'll keep in touch."

Daniel took the only photo he had of himself from his wallet and watched as the rolling hills of Virginia disappeared through the bus window. He glanced at the image of himself as a baby. He was in the arms of some unknown man and the black and white photograph was the only possession he'd grabbed, along with his clothes and money, as he'd quickly packed his bag. Daniel didn't know why he'd taken the photo other than it gave him a history. Putting it away, he wondered just what his future held.

He'd never known any other place, had never even been to another state. He knew there was a big world out there to see but never thought he'd get the chance. Those chances had only been in his dreams. But in one sitting he would see a piece of the world as he made his way to New Mexico. He looked down at the sheet of paper Charley had given him. On it was the name of the person who would offer him a new life.

There it was again. The sound brought Daniel back to the present. It was a scraping noise, as if something was rubbing heavily against the ground, pawing even. It was closer to him, too. Daniel lifted the flashlight once again. The light reached the locked gate to the sanctuary's land. Carefully, he climbed over the gate and softly dropped to the other side. Turning around, he raised the flashlight to the dark.

It took but seconds to see him. There in its full beautiful glory, not six feet from Daniel, stood the elusive ghost stallion. He was big for a mustang, probably sixteen or seventeen hands, but he was definitely part of the wild horse bands of mustangs that roamed freely on the ranch. Daniel had seen him before but only through binoculars. The stallion kept his band of mares "up in the trees", an expression Daniel learned meant staying near a cluster or copse of trees, avoiding contact with humans. The horse probably mistrusted all humans due to the roundups inflicted on many of the herds. It took a lot to win the trust of these incredible animals, but you first had to get close to them. It hadn't been possible with this leader, at least not until now, Daniel thought.

The stallion stood its ground. He watched Daniel cautiously. His wide-set eyes were alert, his withers prominent. Daniel could see the animal's breath being exhaled through its nostrils and imagined he heard it too. His mane and tail were full, and shades much darker than the dun colored coat. Then he noticed the dorsal stripe down the spine, a sign of ancient Spanish blood, further confirming to Daniel that he was facing Espíritu, the Spanish name for ghost or spirit. Daniel had seen that kind of stripe on only a few of the other horses on the ranch. The horse had been tagged by the Bureau of Land Management and the brand was visible on the animal's neck.

Daniel carefully lowered his body to the ground, keeping the beam from the flashlight angled just enough to cast light in the horse's direction. He didn't wish to frighten the animal by shining the light directly into its face. He knelt down, head bowed. The body submission indicated to the horse that Daniel wasn't a threat. Often the horses would be curious and venture closer. The stallion snorted and bobbed his head, pawing the ground again with his hoof. If Daniel hadn't known better, he would've thought the horse was begging, a bad habit some of the domesticated horses on the ranch did when hand-fed too many treats. But Daniel had interrupted the great stallion's grazing and the animal was pawing away the snow to find something to eat.

"I take it you couldn't sleep either," Daniel said quietly to the animal.

The stallion's small ears twitched at the unfamiliar sound and he raised his head. But he didn't move away or venture closer to Daniel. He stood his ground, eyeing Daniel with newfound interest.

"Well, I know how that is. Sometimes you have to get out and just clear your head," Daniel whispered.

The horse stared as if he understood. Daniel couldn't believe this beautiful animal was right before his eyes. No one else would believe it either. This leader was a member of the only band that completely shunned human contact. Some bands were friendlier than others, but this stallion never got within two hundred yards of any person. Until now. Daniel wondered what put him at ease. He also knew that since he was a herd animal, the horse's band family would be nearby, probably watching.

"You are a handsome beast, Espíritu," said Daniel. "You don't mind me calling you that, do you?"

The stallion nodded his head, as if he understood. Daniel slowly raised his arm, with the palm of his hand down, he fisted his hand and stretched as far as he could without moving the rest of his body. It was a connection he was trying to make with the animal. He'd done this many times before with some of the other bands of horses and most of them responded to him by sniffing his hand. Some even let him touch their muzzle. He hoped the same would happen with this special creature.

But the horse wasn't as trusting as the others. He quickly raised his head in response to Daniel's moving arm, keeping the distance between the two of them. He stared at Daniel's hand as if it were something unpleasant. But Daniel didn't move. He kept his arm extended, hoping the animal would trust him.

"C'mon. I won't hurt you. I promise," Daniel coaxed, softly.

Ever so slowly, the giant beast lowered his head. Daniel held his breath. His eyes filled with tears as the horse's lower lip gently touched the top of his hand. He smiled through the tears as the stallion's whiskers tickled his skin and he watched the nostrils working, taking in the scent of his hand. The stallion didn't try to bite him, something that had happened to Daniel before. Instead, the animal was content to sniff.

"That's a good boy. I told you it was okay," he soothed.

Daniel then slid his palm underneath the horse's chin, rubbing the animal gently. How effortless it was surprised him. He'd expected resistance from the great leader. Daniel had been told many times that he had a way with animals, especially horses. But connecting with this animal was unexpected. He wondered again what made the stallion trust him.

"Espíritu, I'm going to stand up now, real easy, so don't get spooked," said Daniel, slowly standing.

The horse lifted its head slightly, ears up and eyes staring at Daniel. He moved to the stallion's left shoulder so the horse could better see him. The animal was on alert, ready to bolt if necessary. A bond of trust was forming between human and animal. If Daniel had learned anything in the three years on the ranch, it was the necessity to respect the animals in order to understand them. Learn their ways and understand the reasons for what they did. Then and only then could you integrate with them and gain their trust.

As Daniel reached his full height, the stallion lifted its head, staring down at him. The movement was to indicate dominance and to let Daniel know there was distance still to keep.

"Okay, I get it. You're still in charge," said Daniel.

Almost immediately, the stallion blew through its nose and backed away, turning his body to trot off into the darkness. Daniel looked at the moon and saw it nearly full and shining in a clear sky. That gave the horse light to see, better helping the band move and graze at night, although they were fully capable of roaming in complete darkness.

Daniel couldn't believe what had just happened. He shined his flashlight in the distance and saw the stallion meeting up with the other horses. He watched as they stood, head and ears alert to any potential threats, and then they started moving. He figured they ventured down out of the trees at night, grazing closer to human contact when it wasn't as likely to happen.

He knew that particular herd was part of the few Pryor Mountain Mustangs brought to the ranch. The Bureau of Land Management had rounded them up and they were offered as adoption to landowners who could provide space for them. The horses were people shy, having endured trauma and harsh conditions by the only people they'd ever come into contact with.

The BLM's practices of rounding up wild horses included the use of helicopters and four-wheelers, terrorizing the animals into captivity. Some of them didn't survive it and the ones that did, were contained in close, cramped pens. Many were separated from the only band family they'd ever known. Some of the pregnant mares would miscarry because of the harshness. They were held until it was decided what to do with them. If they were fortunate, they'd be adopted, like the ones here, Daniel thought. If not, it could mean a trip to the slaughterhouse for any of the poor souls.

Daniel shuddered. He couldn't believe that horse slaughter was once again legal in the country. If only the beauty and spirit of wild horses could be seen by everyone. They belonged in the openness.

He remembered the first time he'd seen a band of wild horses running together. It was the most beautiful thing he'd ever laid eyes on.

Just after he'd arrived at the ranch, Daniel was being shown around by the man Charley said would help him. Frank Carpenter was a tough cowboy. His no-nonsense approach to life contrasted with the sensitivity he showed to the living creatures sharing the ranch. Frank and his wife, Sarah, owned the wild horse sanctuary that Daniel now called home.

"Come with me. I want you to see something," Frank had said to Daniel that day.

He followed the man to the truck and they both got inside. Frank started the engine and they drove, dodging piñon pines and sagebrush. When Daniel thought they must surely be about to drive off the face of the earth, Frank stopped the truck at the base of a small mesa. Getting out of the truck, the man motioned for Daniel to follow him up the slope.

Reaching the flat top, Frank turned to Daniel and pushed the brim of the worn out cowboy hat back from his brow. His face was weathered and tan, his eyes kind.

"When you turn around, you'll see something I bet you've never seen before. If it takes your breath away, then you'll fit in nicely. If you don't feel anything, then maybe you don't belong here," he said.

Daniel turned, allowing his gaze to roam the landscape. His heart caught in his chest. On the other side of the mesa, he looked down at nature in its splendor. Horses of various sizes and colors dotted the terrain. There were two groups of them. Daniel would later learn these were called bands. One band was stationed near a pond, drinking and cooling off from the afternoon heat. A couple of colts ran clumsily around each other, playing and nipping. A foal stayed close to its mother.

The second band was grazing several yards away. Nine or ten horses concerned only with feeding, a few looking up now and then would make sure the other band was keeping its distance. A light-colored horse that looked as if a bucket of dark paint had been splattered on its back decided a roll in the mud would feel nice. That made Daniel smile.

Then one of the horses slowly ventured outside of the circle, as if it were being called over by the other band near the water. He noticed a horse from the opposite band greeting it. They stood there together for a while, as if they were having a chat. Soon the atmosphere changed when the leader of the second band noticed his mare was straying. The stallion charged up to the two horses.

The aggressor lowered his head, moving it side to side in a motion that Daniel would later learn to call "snaking", and ran toward the straying horse. The straggler was chased back to the original band and the angry horse turned to face the third one. All of the other horses watched in anticipation.

"Stallions," Frank said, "they're fightin' over a girl."

Rearing on their back legs, the two stallions faced off at each other. Ears flattened and teeth bared, they fought over territory. Daniel thought if the biting didn't work, then the hooves probably would, as one horse came down on the other one.

"Should we do something?" he asked.

"Nope. They'll work it out," Frank drawled.

Then suddenly, as if an understanding had been reached, the two horses parted and returned to their own bands. Neither one looked too banged up from where Daniel was standing, but he knew he'd witnessed a communication beyond words.

Something caught the horses' attention as each one raised heads and ears to the wind. They'd heard or smelled something they perceived as dangerous and all turned to run. And it was glorious. They moved as one, colors blending together like a painting on canvas. Dust stirred and muscles flexed in the masterpiece, manes and tails flowing freely and wildly. It was the most beautiful thing Daniel had ever seen. And when they were out of sight, he turned to face Frank.

"Well, now. I think you'll do just fine here," Frank said, grinning.

"How do you know?" asked Daniel.

"It's written all over your face," Frank replied.

Daniel returned to the old kiva and sat down, remembering that day. He had been so happy here. Frank and Sarah had taken him in and treated him like a son. Luck had been with him the day Charley walked into his house three years ago. He promised someday he'd repay everyone for the kindness.

His thoughts turned to the withered cottonwood just past the gate to the sanctuary land. The aged tree had been his inspiration of strength and survival during his three years on the ranch. The Carpenters had been his support.

CHAPTER TWO

Frank Carpenter leaned against the rail as he watched Daniel with the new horse. Pride welled in his chest as if the boy were his own son. He'd never seen someone take to these animals as easily and quickly as Daniel Anderson. When Charley had called him three years ago asking a favor, he'd never guessed he would be asked to take a young, broken boy into his home.

Sarah had agreed immediately. They'd never been able to have children of their own and Frank knew it was one thing Sarah wanted more than life itself. Heck, he had wanted it, too. But that was a long time ago. Too many miscarriages and shattered hopes for the future had caused him to grow tired of the wishing. He had moved on from that dream but Sarah hadn't. She wanted a child and didn't care if it came in a teenage package.

Frank reluctantly agreed after hearing the boy's history. He'd never forgive himself if fate threw the kid a fatal blow and Frank hadn't helped in some way. But he and Sarah discussed the difficulties. They didn't know anything other than Daniel's name, age, where he was from and that he came from an abusive home. Those conditions don't always mold the best human beings. They had seen it firsthand with many of the kids on the reservation. Poverty, abuse and alcoholism often lead the teenagers to drugs and crime. He and Sarah agreed at the first sign of trouble, they'd send the boy back to Charley or help find another place for him.

Some of the horrors Daniel had lived through made his skin crawl. He didn't talk about it much, but Charley had eventually given him and Sarah all of the details. Daniel's old man was a bastard and the mother had been a bitch, at least that's the conclusion Frank came to about the woman. Charley still nurtured a soft heart for the dearly departed woman, but Frank felt she was just as bad as her husband. It was probably a good thing his friend had never married her.

Charley Thomas had been Frank's childhood buddy. The two of them grew up together in Colorado and Frank remembered clearly how Charley seemed more of a loner than others he knew. They had become friends in elementary school as a result of fate, more than anything else. Afternoon recess required team selections for kickball and Frank was one of the captains. Of course, the more athletic kids were picked first. When the final few were left, like crumbs no one wanted, Frank laid eyes on Charley waiting with hopeful eyes for someone to call his name and felt sorry for him. Once Frank pointed at him, Charley began a lifelong devotion to being Frank's friend. And Frank genuinely liked Charley. They stayed friends until high school graduation and then Charley's family moved away. They hadn't seen each other in years, but kept in touch on a regular basis. A good thing for Frank and Sarah, otherwise they would never have met Daniel.

Frank knew that Daniel had nightmares. He'd always been a light sleeper and the first time he heard Daniel get up in the middle of the night, Frank thought he was running away. Frank followed him outside. Daniel had been so distressed that he never suspected he was being followed.

That first time Daniel hadn't gone far, just about a hundred yards or so. A little longer would've gotten him to the shelter of the riding arena. But Daniel had stopped as if in a trance and then collapsed suddenly to his knees. The sobs came next. They were deep and guttural, and tore at Frank's heart. He wanted to rush to Daniel's side and pull the boy into his arms. Frank wanted to reassure Daniel that he was safe and nothing would harm him. But he couldn't. Something told him he'd risk the trust he wanted to have with Daniel. It was important that Daniel know Frank was there for him.

After that, Frank didn't follow Daniel in the middle of the night anymore. But he took extra caution in the way he interacted with the young man in their care. It was important that Daniel like him. Frank hoped Daniel had enough experience with other people to know most folks weren't like his parents. But only time would tell. All Frank could do was be there for him. And he had been every step of the way.

From riding a horse to driving a car, and everything in between, Frank taught Daniel with patience and kindness, taking great pride in every small step of success. Sarah saw it, too. She remarked once on how she thought Frank had rescued Daniel's fragile soul.

"What do you mean?" Frank had asked.

"I think you look at Daniel as a son we never had. That makes me happy." She had smiled as she said it and wrapped her arms around his waist.

"I think you're right, as usual," he replied, kissing the top of her head.

He and Sarah had been together forever it seemed. They were college sweethearts and he still felt about her the same way he had the first time he saw her way back then. He loved her with all his being. And she loved him.

They had come far together and they'd made a nice life, starting out with very little. Everyone told them they should wait to get married but marriage came right after college graduation. In the beginning, they worked any job they could get just to get them through the lean years of skimping and saving and doing without if it cost too much. Sarah worked with special education students until his career sent them down another path.

Frank got his first full time job out of college as a wrangler for a Colorado rancher. He received a degree in Equine Studies knowing he wanted to devote his life to caring for and managing horses. While school gave him the degree, on the job training proved to be an invaluable investment in his future. He learned every little quirk and trait associated with each horse on that ranch. After a while, it was easy to know the mood or temperament simply by looking at the horse. He learned how to train them and he learned how to manage them. Most of all he respected them and they returned the favor.

Another job took him and Sarah to northern New Mexico. He worked for a rancher there for a number of years, managing and training the herd of horses the man owned. Eventually, he and Sarah had saved enough to buy a small piece of land nearby. There was a cabin on the property they moved into and for the next several years they tried to have children.

After about the third miscarriage, Frank was ready to give up. He couldn't stand how it was affecting Sarah. He'd wanted kids, but his wife was more important to him. Plus, he knew they could adopt. God knew there were enough neglected children who needed them. But Sarah was determined. She wanted to have their child.

So the hopeful promise followed by extreme disappointment continued until his wife's gynecologist finally said she couldn't try anymore. Her health wouldn't allow it. Frank promised Sarah they would then look into adopting. But all attempts at that had failed miserably.

Their first choice had been a newborn, but newborns didn't come up for adoption very often so they had been placed on a waiting list. In the meantime, many older children came through their doors and none of them stayed. All were returned to a foster or birth family for various reasons: a change of heart by the birth family or a problem child who didn't want to stay with them. Frank resigned himself to the fact they'd never have children. Sarah never did.

She eventually started keeping books for Frank's aging employer. It was a job once held by the man's late wife that he readily handed to Sarah when the woman died. The rancher had made a fortune in the oil and cattle business in Texas but grief brought him and his wife to New Mexico after they lost their teenage daughter to cancer. They decided to change direction and start a horse ranch.

The man had been giving Frank more responsibility running the property as his health deteriorated too. It was a lot of work but Frank appreciated the experience. The rancher had a few thousand acres and devoted most of it to horse management and breeding. Frank thought there might be an opportunity to expand and utilize all of the land in some capacity, possibly growing their own hay, or by teaching natural horsemanship to those willing to learn it, a specialty he believed in and lived by.

The rancher never saw those ideas to fruition as he died before plans were realized. Frank was then forced to face his own future. He'd hoped that whoever inherited or bought the ranch would keep him on but he knew that wasn't a guarantee.

It was a worry that wasn't necessary. He and Sarah had been left everything. The ranch house, all of the land and the horses. It belonged to them and it took a long time to get over the shock. Years passed before they stopped wondering if someone, a long lost heir perhaps, would show up and challenge the will. No one ever did. They worked, built and expanded their holdings into a reputable and respected business. They bought real estate and eventually got out of the horse breeding business. And they never took any of it for granted.

They didn't sell their first home, opting instead to purchase the few acres between it and the ranch. The small cabin held too much sentimental value for them to get rid of it. In fact, they continued living in the cabin for some time after the ranch became theirs. Finally, one day Sarah announced that it was time to move. And they did. Frank didn't know why it took them so long to accept the larger ranch house as their own. Maybe it was out of respect for the man that had been so generous with them. At any rate, they made it their home and never looked back.

Frank watched Daniel. He'd turned into a young man in such a short amount of time. Before him stood a tall, muscular and confident looking person, someone comfortable with what life had to offer. What a contrast to the sad, flinching form that met Frank three years prior. He listened as Joe tried teasing Daniel about meeting the ghost horse.

"Well, did he scare you then?" asked Joe.

"I was a little scared before I knew what it was," replied Daniel.

"But you weren't scared of a ghost?" Joe asked.

"It wasn't a ghost," Daniel said patiently, "it was a horse."

"But you thought it was at first," replied Joe.

"No, I didn't know what it was. I just heard a noise," Daniel said.

"I always think noises belong to ghosts," shivered Joe.

"Why?" Daniel asked.

"Because I live on a reservation," exclaimed Joe, "and every time someone turns around, they're warding off evil spirits."

"Isn't that to protect you?" Daniel asked.

"I guess so. It doesn't make for easy sleeping at night though," sighed Joe.

Daniel laughed. "Hey, you have all those dream catchers to hang from the windows."

"Nope. A different tribe adopted that crazy idea. But we still have our own mad as a hatter beliefs," Joe shook his head.

Daniel smiled at the younger boy. "You should appreciate all of that."

"I do. It just always keeps me on edge. And if I hear something and can't see it, I'll naturally think it's a ghost. And why did you call the horse 'Ghost'?"

"Espíritu," corrected Daniel.

"Whatever," continued Joe, rolling his eyes. "It still means the same thing. It's creepy."

"It just came to me, I guess," Daniel said.

"You mean it didn't neigh first and then say 'boo'?" he laughed, trying to mimic the sound of a horse.

Frank watched and smiled as the two of them laughed. Daniel's laughter was deep and seemed to come from his heart. Joe's laugh was still child-like and innocent and sure to change in the coming year or so. Daniel was only a couple of years older than Joe, but the age difference seemed greater. Physically, Joe was slight. His clothes hung from a thin frame and he looked underweight. However, he could also eat his weight in food, never gaining an ounce, as Frank and Sarah would watch in amusement whenever he ate with them.

Joe was well taken care of, a fact Frank knew as Joe's parents worked on the ranch. There weren't two harder working individuals than Inez and Bill. And Frank trusted them. He didn't hesitate turning over the reins, so to speak, to Bill whenever it was needed. The man had more horse sense than most and Inez proved to be invaluable to Sarah.

His thoughts turned to the horse sanctuary and how Bill had helped him start it. Bill often talked of just how many wild mustangs roamed the endless expanse of reservation land. While Frank hadn't been a champion of the BLM, he knew the mustangs on the reservations weren't protected by any US laws and there were limits to what the BLM could do because of such laws on US soil. Plus, he knew many of the horses on the reservations were starving because of a depleted rangeland. A lack of involvement by tribal leaders and overbreeding within the horse herds were to blame.

Wild horses rounded up on reservations could be sold, neglected and abused. Many found their way to the rodeo circuit as bronco horses. Frank tolerated rodeos since most folks he knew enjoyed them, but he felt some operated on borderline cruelty. Sarah outright refused to go to a rodeo and Frank knew Daniel didn't favor them very much.

It was Bill who arranged the bargaining when Frank expressed an interest in providing a home to the displaced creatures. He had the land and it seemed a shame to do nothing. So, with Bill, he attended his first wild horse auction and it turned his stomach.

What greeted him existed on the lowest rung of the horse business. While the horses were going for ridiculously low prices, he watched helplessly as foals were separated from their mothers. Dazed and scared colts were purchased by the stock buyers, their future left to the mercy of the rodeo circuit. But the worst fate belonged to those selected by the kill buyers. The heartless were interested in the horses that would fetch the greatest amount of money based on weight. Then the poor souls were transported to the slaughterhouse, with the kill buyers being paid for the meat. At least for a while, the slaughterhouses in this country were shut down. Not so anymore.

Frank was able to acquire several horses that day. His heart wanted to buy all of them. But these few creatures formed the foundation of his and Sarah's sanctuary and every time he thought about that auction, it made his blood boil. He swore as long as he was standing and able, he'd do everything in his power to raise awareness for the plight of the wild mustang. He felt it was the right thing to do, and something had to be done to protect what was considered a part of the country's national heritage.

So he'd fought the Bureau of Land Management, arguing against roundups on open and public rangeland. Their argument was that the horses were desecrating the natural habitat. He countered by saying cattle did more damage than horses. Frank suspected some in the BLM to be on the sides of the cattle ranchers and oil companies, both wanting to have access to the public land via lease rights for their own gain. And roaming and grazing wild horses stood in their way.

Fortunately, laws protected the wild horse on US soil but the increasing herd sizes allowed the BLM to come up with a way to control the herds. Thus, the roundups. Younger, healthier horses were re-released into the wild and the rest were sold. Auctions were held for the captured ones, but unlike the auctions held on the reservations, prices were higher and the buyers had to prove they had acreage for the horses and were able to care for them. Some of the horses weren't adopted and they were kept in captivity, their living conditions questionable and their fates uncertain.

Frank knew that was the BLM's way of controlling herd population. There'd be fewer horses in the wild. He had argued in support of contraception. They used it on the horses at his sanctuary and he admitted it didn't always take, but it did often enough. And it was better than nothing. It was expensive and tricky, involving the use of a dart projector to shoot the mare in the hindquarters with the contraceptive. When the needle stuck, the injection was quick and automatic. The dart released itself from the horse after injection, to be retrieved or lost in the terrain. On occasion, the mares that were given the contraceptive turned up pregnant. This didn't discourage Frank's belief in using contraception because his herd population had been under control for a number of years.

His stance on the wild horse issue caused him to make a few enemies. There were some ranchers who were upset with him for creating the sanctuary so close to their own lands. They wanted nothing to do with wild horses, fearing unrealistically that if any of them got off Frank's land and on theirs, damage to their property would be automatic.

"Whoa, boy. Take it easy," Daniel said, bringing Frank's attention to the present.

The horse was spirited and had started bucking. The gelding was acquired from a man Frank knew who tried saving horses from the local rodeo grind. This particular horse had proved no use to the circuit and was deemed unusable and untrainable. No one knew where the animal had come from but Frank suspected it had once been wild. And since it was a gelding, it had probably been captured by the BLM as a colt, and then auctioned when it was old enough.

"Maybe you should get out of his way," Joe said nervously, fidgeting as he sat on the rail.

"I've got it under control," replied Daniel, confidently.

"But he looks like he's got enough sass in him to send you flying if he wanted," said Joe.

"He probably does, but I don't think he wants to," Daniel said.

"How do you know these things? It's like you can read a horse's mind or something," Joe said.

"It's just something I know," said Daniel.

"And it's not just horses," continued Joe, "dogs, too. You know what Bob wants before he does." At the sound of his name, Bob the dog, who had been lounging under a shade tree, sat up and cocked his head to one side.

"You just have to listen and watch, Joe. That's all," Daniel replied.

"I do listen. I just can't hear it," said Joe.

"When I first met you, it took forever before you said a word. Now you won't stop talking," laughed Daniel, his eyes never leaving the horse.

"I had a lot of catching up to do," said Joe.

Frank watched as the horse pranced around Daniel, who was using a lunge line to work the animal. Its head was held high, tail and mane moving in rhythm. Frank knew by the horse's body language it wasn't a threat to Daniel. The ears were up, not flat, and the nostrils weren't pinched. This guy viewed Daniel as a curiosity, maybe even a challenge. Funny, Frank thought, because he knew Daniel probably felt the same about the gelding.

Daniel stood with one arm down at his side, the other holding the lunge line, in the center of the arena. He turned as the horse moved, never taking his eyes from the animal. The gelding would buck every now and then, neighing and squealing, as if trying to send a message that said, "back off". Daniel never wavered. He was patient, hopefully sending the message that he wouldn't be intimidated. The prancing continued until finally the horse decided he'd venture a little closer to the human.

It was Daniel's goal to simply touch the animal first, something not many had been able to do successfully. Frank suspected no one had taken the time to desensitize it, never following through with basic groundwork needed to train a horse. As far as he could tell, the animal had never been trained enough to even saddle it properly, much less ride it. They had tried to release it onto the sanctuary grounds to see if it would join with one of the herds, but the gelding kept coming back to the house, waiting to be fed some hay.

This eventually caused Daniel to start calling the horse "Misfit" because it simply didn't belong anywhere. It was once wild, but no longer wished to be. At the same time, it acted wild around people and the domesticated horses on the ranch, probably because of inconsistent training and bad experiences with humans.

Frank watched as the horse crept toward Daniel. It lowered its head for just a fraction, then quickly raised it as if he'd realized he was relaxing and wasn't ready yet. Daniel slowly moved to the left side of the horse's head and raised his left hand so the animal could sniff. He carefully lifted his right arm to gently touch the horse's neck with his other hand. The animal didn't flinch and Daniel spoke soothingly to it, his voice caressing as much as his hand was.

"That's a good boy, Misfit," he whispered to the animal. "We're not so different, you and I."

Daniel touched as long as the horse allowed, then as if the animal had had enough, it turned and strode toward the rail. Daniel quickly backed away, anticipating a kick that never came. He watched as the horse pranced, a little less lively than before, but still possessing an alertness that indicated he didn't quite trust yet.

Frank knew it was just a matter of time before Daniel would have him saddled and ready to ride. Old Misfit didn't stand a chance, thought Frank, smiling to himself.

"Hey, when are you going to try seeing the ghost horse again?" asked Joe.

"Oh, I don't know. It's not something you can plan," said Daniel.

"Why not? " Joe asked.

"You can see him anytime you want up in the trees. Just get some binoculars," smiled Daniel.

"That's not what I mean. You know, up close. When are you going to see him up close again, Daniel?" he asked.

"Just because you plan on seeing him doesn't mean you will. It's up to him," Daniel stated.

"But you have to make yourself available," sighed Joe.

"Why do you want to know anyway?" Daniel asked.

"Because I want to see him, too. Do you think I can?" asked Joe.

"I don't see why not," Daniel said, watching the horse slow down.

"You mean it? Really? I thought you'd say no," said Joe.

"Why?" asked Daniel, surprised.

"Well, I'm not exactly an animal magnet. I don't have the gift like you," Joe said.

"That doesn't have anything to do with whether we'll see the horse or not," Daniel replied.

"I know, but I could bring you bad luck, if you think about it. If the horse senses I'm there, he might stay away," said Joe.

"I doubt it, Joe. But if you keep talking like that, you might talk yourself out of the chance to come along," laughed Daniel.

"Well, I'll shut up then. Do you think we could try tonight?" he asked.

"I guess we could, if I can borrow the truck," Daniel said, glancing at Frank.

"Fine with me," said Frank, still watching the horse.

"So you'll pick me up?" Joe asked Daniel.

"I figured I would," Daniel replied.

"Uh, one problem, though," Joe began, "I'm helping my uncle at the Turnout. Can you pick me up there?"

Daniel said that he could and Frank once again marveled at the light Daniel had brought to his and Sarah's lives. He would be forever grateful to his friend, Charley, for making that phone call three years ago. He would also go to the ends of the earth to see that Daniel never suffered another day of his life.

CHAPTER THREE

Daniel pulled into the gravel parking lot of the Turnout. Joe's uncle, Merrill, owned the restaurant and bar that was located on the outskirts of the reservation. In the last year, Joe had been helping out, doing any odd job his uncle needed for him to do. It wasn't one of Daniel's favorite places to go. Too many people wasting money they didn't have getting drunk, simply because life left them behind. It brought back memories he didn't like remembering.

Getting out of the truck, Daniel looked up at the clear night sky. It should make for an easier time to search for Espíritu's band of horses. He'd take Joe back to the kiva. That would be the best starting place.

He opened the door to the bar and his eyes had to adjust. The neon signs advertising beer blinked through the haze of cigarette smoke. His eyes and nostrils burned. Music blared from the jukebox, some song about cowboys and the women who cheated on them. Most of the occupants were sitting around or leaning against the bar, since there weren't many tables and all were occupied. He didn't see Joe anywhere.

"Hey, Daniel! Good to see you," said Joe's uncle, from behind him.

"Hi, Merrill. Good to see you, too," replied Daniel, turning to see the man, and grasping his extended hand. He smiled at Merrill's round face. He was a short man who wore his hair long and tied back with a thin piece of leather. His existence had been hard and he wore the life wounds on his body for all to see. Stooped and scarred, the man had survived polio as a child and a severe case of chicken pox late in life that almost killed him. A divorce he hadn't wanted had been difficult and the worry from it left shadows of sadness and failure in his demeanor.

"Joe's on the other side, working in the dining room," Merrill said. "You can go on over if you'd like."

"Thanks," said Daniel, as he moved toward the entrance of the restaurant area, just past the bar.

He made his way into the dining room, where he was able to breathe a little better. The lighting was preferable, too. Most people had finished eating by that time and all but a couple of tables were empty. He saw Joe in the back, bussing a table.

"Working hard?" he asked, walking up to his friend.

"Not so much. It's been a slow night. Most people are in the bar," Joe replied, wiping the table.

"Hey, Joe. Where did you say these are stored?" asked a female voice from behind Daniel.

Daniel turned to see who owned the voice. When he did it felt like the wind had been knocked out of him. He was sure the whole restaurant heard his gasp. Standing there was a girl about his age with the complexion of an angel. Her hair was dark and her eyes, tinged with long, thick eyelashes, were a soft brown. She wore little earrings that seemed to move on their own. Dragging his eyes from her face, Daniel noticed she had on jeans, a sweatshirt and in her arms she held a large box. He knew he should say something but he couldn't find his voice. It had deserted him and all he could do was stare. Daniel hoped his mouth wasn't gaping open.

"Just leave them on the table. I'll put them away," Joe replied.

It was then that Daniel found his mobility. Reaching for the box she held, he croaked, "Here let me help you." He hoped it didn't sound like squawking but thought it probably did. Joe confirmed it.

"What's wrong with your voice?" he asked, a little loudly, Daniel thought.

"N-nothing," Daniel stammered, clearing his voice and looking at the girl. "I'm Daniel."

"Hi. I'm Maria," she replied, with a smile.

Her smile could light up all of New Mexico he thought, staring at her straight teeth. What was wrong with him? Time seemed to stand still and he was right in the middle of it. His brain was working faster than anything else would. He felt his face flushing and he hoped Maria didn't notice.

"You going to stand there all day with the box?" Joe asked, looking at Daniel closely.

"Where did you say to leave it?" Daniel asked, recovering.

"I said just leave it on the table, but since you're big and strong, you can place it on that top shelf," Joe replied, pointing above Daniel's head.

Daniel lifted the box and slid it carefully onto the shelf. He took a deep breath and turned around to face Maria and Joe, but his eyes lingered on Maria. It was like a thirst being quenched. His vision couldn't get enough of her face.

"Well, here we are, standing in the middle of the Turnout," said Joe, rubbing his hands together.

Daniel noticed the sarcasm and ignored it. He admitted to still being at a loss for words but he had reclaimed his senses somewhat. It appeared Maria might be as nervous as he was, but he wasn't sure if that was a good sign.

"Hello, earth to Daniel. Are we going or not? You could ask Maria if she wants to go," Joe hinted.

"Go where?" asked Maria.

Before Daniel could answer, Joe continued. "To find the ghost horse."

Confusion, mixed with a little fear, flashed across Maria's face, causing Daniel to explain. "He's part of a band of horses living on our land that won't have anything to do with people. I came across them the other night and Joe wants to try to find the herd again."

"I want to see the leader. Espíritu," Joe said.

"Espíritu?" asked Maria.

"Yes, that's what I call him," said Daniel. "You can come along if you'd like."

"I would like to," she replied, her eyes shining.

Some unseen force muted Daniel's voice again. His arms and legs felt too heavy to move. Maria wanted to come along and all he could do was stand there stupidly and stare. How could he make it through the night with her riding in his truck? Hell, he wasn't even sure he'd be able to drive much less make it outside.

"Good grief," Joe said, shaking his head. "Can we leave?"

"Sure," Daniel murmured.

Somehow he found his legs and they walked outside to his truck. Maria slid in the middle, between Daniel and Joe. Daniel could smell the clean scent of her shampoo, mixed a little with the odor of the restaurant and bar. On her, it wasn't an offensive smell. It was kind of nice he thought. Occasionally as he drove, his right arm would brush her left one. Even wearing jackets, the action sent shivers down his spine. Her long hair also kept sweeping over his arm as she turned her head and it fell forward. He still hadn't said much and didn't know if he was capable.

"Nice weather we're having," Joe murmured, drumming his fingers on the dashboard.

That made Maria laugh. It was the sweetest sound Daniel had ever heard. It reminded him of happiness, innocence and a carefree trust unknown to someone like Daniel. He liked the sound and wanted to hear more of it.

"Oh, Joey, you've always been the funny and clever one," said Maria.

"Joey?" asked Daniel, in surprise.

"That's what we called him when we were little," she responded.

"So you're related?" Daniel asked.

"Cousins. And you can call me Joe. Remember that," Joe replied.

"Oh, I remember, all right. Joey," Daniel smiled.

They drove into the night and Daniel relaxed. He was able to carry on a logical conversation and discovered Maria was Merrill's daughter. A long, lost one who hadn't visited her father much over the years. Her parents' divorce had caused bad feelings between the two people she loved the most, and forced Maria to live with her mother in Colorado. It wasn't until she turned eighteen that she was able to tell her mother that she was going to visit her father because she wanted to. She wished to get to know the man and to understand the culture that was important to him.

Daniel drove as close as he could to the kiva and parked the truck. He grabbed the flashlight, telling Maria and Joe to follow him. As an afterthought, he reminded Maria to zip her jacket so she wouldn't get cold, and then regretted it. Did he really just say that? He waited for Joe's wisecrack, but it didn't come.

Shining the light on their surroundings and in the distance, the three of them slipped through the sanctuary's gate. Daniel found no trace of the horses. It didn't mean the herd wouldn't show up later. They could wait around for a while and see.

"This place gives me the creeps," Joe murmured.

"You wanted to see Espíritu, Joe. This is where I saw him," said Daniel.

"It still gives me the creeps," Joe replied.

"It's just because of the kiva, Joey. This is our heritage, you know. The Anasazi," Maria said.

"Too much spiritual stuff in our heritage for my taste," Joe said.

"Our beliefs protect us," she said.

"Our beliefs blind us sometimes," Joe replied.

"If we didn't have our beliefs, we'd forget our past. Remembering our past helps us change the future," said Maria.

Daniel looked at Maria. His heart felt like it would burst out of his chest. He'd spent his life trying to forget his past in hopes of a better tomorrow. But if he didn't remember, how could he consciously change things for the better? She was right and he wanted to kiss her right then and there. She looked at him then, as if she sensed it, too.

"Do you hear something?" Joe asked, breaking the trance.

They listened but heard nothing. Daniel moved the flashlight's beam around but it seemed they were the only beings out in that area. Probably a good thing, Daniel thought, as the only living creatures he'd really want to encounter there at night would be the horses.

"This is where I first met you, Joe. Remember?" Daniel reminded his friend.

"I remember. It was daylight though. No chance of ghostly encounters then," replied Joe.

"I thought you wanted a ghostly encounter," Daniel said.

"Of the real horsey kind, not some dead ancestor who is pissed off because the automobile was invented," Joe said.

"Well, I can't guarantee either one," replied Daniel.

"Are you sure your ghost horse was real? I mean we're near this ceremonial place, it could've been some conjured up, long ago war horse," breathed Joe.

"It was alive and breathing, as sure as we're standing here. Trust me," Daniel said.

"How do you know it was your up in the trees herd?" asked Joe.

"Because I've watched that band through binoculars for months. That stallion is distinctive," Daniel said. "Plus, I know all the other herds here on the ranch. There aren't any others."

"Daniel, look," said Maria softly. She took his hand in hers. Her touch was silky and it made him inhale quickly. It took great effort for him to stop staring at their intertwined hands and look where she wanted. He also consciously had to exhale because he felt lightheaded, realizing he'd been holding his breath.

Daniel raised the flashlight and standing in front of them was what appeared to be a weanling. The light seemed to startle the youngster, so Daniel lowered it, hoping its eyes would adjust. He also knew not to approach the animal because the dam would be nearby, which also meant the herd was somewhere close. The weanling's silliness and curiosity probably caused it to wander off. In the wild, that could be dangerous. He just hoped the animal hadn't wandered too far from its herd. Daniel knew he wouldn't be able to leave it to its own defenses.

He didn't have to worry, at least not about it being alone. Within seconds, the weanling was joined by its mama and she didn't look too happy. Her head was low and he didn't have to see the rest of her features to read her mood. He was pretty certain the two horses were part of the elusive herd they'd been waiting to see. A sudden neigh came from the dark, high in pitch but dropping suddenly in tone. The mare's head came up, as did her ears. The whinny served its purpose. The two horses moved as one, backing into the darkness and away from them.

Daniel lifted the light and saw the rest of the band, staggered like statues on the landscape. It was a large herd. He counted about twelve horses. In the front, closest to them, stood Espíritu, tall and proud. The stallion stared back and Daniel felt the horse remembered him. He seemed more curious than fearful. The other horses waited for their leader's cue, and finally it was given. A soft nickering was made from the great stallion and all of the horses turned as Espíritu did, with relaxed bodies. They grazed in spots and within minutes, decided it was time to move on, not in a frightened gallop, but in a slow trot. Espíritu let the herd know that Daniel wasn't a threat.

They watched until the band was out of sight and stood quietly for minutes afterward. No one wished to break the silence but it was Joe who finally did.

"That was awesome," he breathed.

"I'll make a horse lover out of you yet," Daniel smiled.

"I doubt it, but it was still awesome," Joe replied.

"Was the one in the front your Espíritu?" asked Maria.

"Yes. Wasn't he beautiful?"

Maria nodded, her eyes bright. Daniel noticed they were still holding hands and it seemed the most natural thing to do. He didn't want the night to end.

"You know, I knew he'd show up," Joe said.

"Well, you didn't sound too confident earlier," laughed Daniel.

"It's just the surroundings and the night. I let my emotions get carried away," he replied.

"It happens to the best of us," Daniel said.

They walked back to the truck, saying very little. The experience had moved them and it seemed words lessened what they had witnessed. Daniel drove Joe home first as his house was farther away. Backtracking, Maria would be dropped off last, as Merrill's house was closer, not far from the Turnout. Daniel didn't mind as it allowed him some time alone with Maria.

After saying goodnight to Joe, they rode in silence, and then awkwardly began talking at once. Laughing, Daniel told Maria to go first.

"It's just that you've done miracles with Joe," Maria said.

"What do you mean?" he asked.

"He's been terrified of horses ever since he was a little kid," she said. "He had a bad fall learning to ride."

"I had no idea. Was he hurt?" Daniel asked.

"Yes, broke his arm and crushed his foot because the horse stepped on it. He was in a lot of pain for a long time," she replied.

"He's never mentioned it. I wondered why he never really got close to the horses, but he's always around when I'm working with them. Is that how he got the limp?" Daniel asked.

"Yes. I think he admires you for what you can do with the horses. And you've given him a little confidence again," Maria said.

"Do you ride?" he asked suddenly.

"Yes, I do, actually," she replied.

"Let me guess. English saddle and dressage?" he asked, with a twinkle in his eye.

"Nope. I'm a cowgirl at heart. Give me that western saddle any day," she laughed.

He told her of his life then. His painful past that he hadn't shared with anyone other than Frank and Sarah. Joe didn't even know. He told her how he came to the ranch three years earlier and had never been around a horse before that, much less ridden or trained one. But it had all come naturally to him. Being on a horse was second nature and it was a freedom he couldn't explain. He talked until he couldn't talk anymore and Maria listened. Then it happened. The one thing he'd thought about earlier.

As he pulled in front of Merrill's house, he turned to Maria. She leaned over and kissed him. If fireworks could go off in his head, then they surely did. The feel of her lips on his own left him senseless. They were soft and firm at the same time, and the feeling made Daniel weak.

It seemed an eternity before he came back to earth and realized their lips were no longer touching. He opened his eyes. Maria's eyes were still closed and he noticed a tiny scar just above her left eyebrow.

It made her even more beautiful he thought. Finally, she looked at him through hooded eyes.

"Daniel, I'm happy I met you," she said.

"Me, too. I mean, I'm happy I met you, too," he replied.

"Do you believe in fate?" she asked.

"I'm not so sure," he said.

"I usually think we control our own destiny, but tonight was magical. Like some force caused things to happen," she said.

"When Charley intervened in my life, maybe fate had something to do with it. I certainly didn't. But I know what you mean about tonight," he smiled.

"Well, I should go in," said Maria. "Do you think we could do this again sometime?"

"I'd like that," he said.

Maria smiled and Daniel walked her to the door. He wondered about fate as he drove home that night. A chain reaction of good came from Charley's visit. He guessed fate had a hand in it. But was it fate that when doling out parents, he'd gotten the rotten apples of the bunch? If so, why? Why does fate smile on some and frown on others? Does it make the disadvantaged stronger? He wondered what road or path he would've taken if Charley hadn't stopped by that night. It would have been harder for him that's for certain. He's thankful he'd never have to find out.

His thoughts turned to Maria. He had never had a crush before if that's what he was experiencing. There were pretty and interesting girls but his life had been such a mess, that he hadn't thought much about them. His only concern for the first fifteen years of his life was about survival then the last three had been about healing. This was all new to him. It scared him but at the same time he looked forward to seeing her again. What he didn't understand was how he became a bowl of mush around her. Maybe that's what made it special but he certainly wished for a little more control.

He smiled thinking of how Frank acted around Sarah sometimes. There were times he'd catch Frank staring at her with such love written all over his face that he knew the man would go to the end of the earth and back for his wife. It was something he'd never witnessed until he had met them. He also liked the bond that Frank and Sarah shared. They seemed to know exactly what the other was thinking before anything was ever said. He could only hope to have that kind of relationship someday.

When Daniel reached his house, he sat staring at the place he called home. Three years earlier, he would never believe he'd ever live in a place like this. He loved it here and he loved the Carpenters. He'd even thought about changing his last name to theirs. Yes, fate intervened that day. He just wished fate would keep the nightmares away.

CHAPTER FOUR

Frank drank his coffee slowly, savoring the taste and needing the jolt to face the day. He dreaded the meeting that morning. His neighbor was up in arms again about the sanctuary and wanted to meet with him. The man was nothing but a hot head, always looking for something to complain about. His son was just like him, too. Trouble followed him wherever he went. Both of them claim one of the bands had crossed over into their pasture. But when Frank rode all along the property line, there was no sign of damage to the fencing. It was high enough that the horses couldn't jump it and he'd installed electric fencing years ago. It was still working. There's no way their claim could be true, but knowing them, they'd find some way of trying to prove it.

He was also facing a potential buyer for the young thoroughbred they'd raised and trained. Daniel had started working with the horse as a weanling not long after his arrival on the ranch. Now it was time to let the horse go. Cyan was the last domesticated horse born on the ranch.

"Aren't you eating any breakfast?" Sarah asked as she entered the kitchen.

"I'm not hungry for some reason. I think I'm just dreading the encounter with old man Tate," he replied, as Sarah kissed the top of his head.

"He's just a sourpuss, you know that. Scrooge has nothing on him," she said.

"I know. It's still unpleasant," he replied, smiling at his wife.

"Well, don't get too upset with him. He seems to have too much pull around here sometimes," Sarah said.

"That's the problem. And because of that, too many people are afraid of him," Frank sighed.

"No one wants to get on his bad side," Sarah replied.

"I know. I still can't help thinking he has something up his sleeve," said Frank.

"He probably does, but we'll figure it out. We always do," she soothed.

"Yeah," he said, pulling Sarah onto his lap. "You are good for me. I already feel better just because of you."

"Well, back at ya', cowboy. We are good for each other," she said, putting her arms around his neck.

He pulled her close. It never ceased to amaze him how her quiet encouragement always put him at ease. He breathed in the clean scent of her. It was so comforting and familiar, yet it held a promise of surprise. They never tired of each other.

"By the way, have you noticed Daniel's been mighty chipper lately? What's the story?" he asked.

"He's in love," she breathed into his ear.

"What?" he asked, pulling away to look at her.

"Yes, Merrill's daughter, Maria. You know, Joe's cousin," Sarah replied.

"Well, I'll be damned. How do you know these things?" Frank asked.

"You men. Life would pass you by if it weren't for us women reminding you to take a look every once in a while," she said.

"That would probably be right," Frank said, laughing out loud. He kissed her fully on the lips as Daniel entered the kitchen. He had been out working.

"Don't let me interrupt," he said, smiling at the two of them.

"Trust me, we won't," Frank said.

"Want some breakfast, Daniel?" Sarah asked.

"Already had some earlier, thank you though," he replied.

"What got you out working so early?" Frank asked.

"I couldn't sleep. Thought I'd go out and work with Cyan a little bit since you might be selling him today," Daniel said.

"Well, I hope to sell him. He'll bring in a nice price and the man will provide a good home for him," Frank said.

"I was wondering if I could go with you to meet the Tates this morning," Daniel said to Frank.

"Certainly. I'd welcome it quite honestly," Frank replied.

"I know you've been dreading it. I just thought I could give moral support," he said.

"Well, there's always strength in numbers that's for sure. Plus, it would mean a lot if you went," said Frank.

"Okay, let me go take a quick shower and I'll be ready," Daniel replied. He left the room and they heard him take the stairs in three quick strides.

"I'm glad he's going. I wish I could," Sarah said.

"I know you do, but I'm glad you're not. Tate can say some pretty insulting things. Plus, you have your meeting," Frank said to his wife, hugging her.

"I could reschedule it, you know," she said.

"I love you for offering, but it isn't necessary. It's more important you go today. It could mean funding for those kids," Frank said.

"I love you, too," she whispered to her husband. Sarah held him close. He was her rock and she was going to need him more than ever if her suspicions proved true. Granted, she was meeting with the state coordinator for a non-profit that could help with some needed funding for an idea she had. She wanted to start an equine therapy program for children with developmental disabilities and physical limitations. She had discussed the idea with some physical therapists in the area, along with other specialists including physicians and special education teachers. The hope was also to draw from the reservation when needed.

However, the meeting wasn't causing the preoccupation that nagged her. That afternoon she had another appointment. It was one she hadn't shared with Frank because she knew he would've insisted on coming, too. She didn't want to worry him. God knows they'll have enough to worry about if it turns out a certain way.

"Okay, I'm ready if you are," Daniel said, freshly showered and shaved, as he came back into the kitchen. His wet blond hair was combed back to air dry. Sarah marveled at how light it was. In the sunlight, his hair appeared so pale that it looked almost white. What women do to their locks to get that color, she thought.

"Well, let's go and get this over with," Frank said, kissing his wife once more. "I'll see you in a while."

Minutes later, he and Daniel were driving along the gravel road saying little but enjoying the sunshine and warmer temperature. Spring had finally made an appearance and it looked as if the earth was awakening from a long slumber. Birds darted low and quick, frantic in their nest building, stopping occasionally to splash in the puddles that dotted the road.

"Mr. Tate doesn't seem to like you much. Why is that?" Daniel asked suddenly.

"You know Sarah and I inherited our land, right?" Frank asked.

"Yes," Daniel nodded. They had shared their history with him shortly after his arrival at the ranch.

"Well, Tate thought he would be able to get this land at auction. Since his property borders it, he would've been quite the land baron if he had," Frank said.

"So he resents that you got it instead," Daniel added.

"Very much so. He never once thought it would be willed to anyone, much less us. We didn't either for that matter," said Frank.

"But why hold such a grudge? It's been a long time," Daniel said.

"Some people can't let things go, and he's one of them. I sometimes think he's made it his life's ambition to give me headaches," Frank smiled.

"Well, if it's any comfort, I think the same thing of his son," Daniel mused.

"You watch out for him," Frank said sharply. "That kid is rotten to the core."

"I figured that out a long time ago. Just can't understand people having so much but doing so little with it," said Daniel.

"Has he done something to you?" Frank asked.

"Not directly. He's made some snide comments about me here and there. I just ignore it. Mostly his cruelty is directed at Joe," Daniel said.

"Let me know when it happens again," Frank said. "And don't let anything he says or does get to you because that's what he wants."

They reached the gate of the Tate ranch. It was ornate and pretentious, with wrought iron embellishments of horses, cowboy hats and a branding iron with the letter "T". The gate was open in anticipation of their arrival and they drove through it, the cattle guard rattling as they crossed. The long drive rose to the rancher's house, an adobe inspired dwelling with several casitas flanking the main residence. It was a contrast to Frank and Sarah's expanse, a traditional looking stick-built house complete with columns and shutters.

The landscaping was nature inspired and blended with the surroundings. There weren't any potted plants to be found. That was something Sarah wouldn't stand for, Frank thought. He knew she was already itching to get started with her flower gardens. The Carpenters utilized the streams and ponds on their land, along with well water, to irrigate, helping not only with the pastures and the horses but also with her gardening. It solved watering restrictions and drought, brought about by the dryer climate.

Ed Tate strode across the drive to greet them. He was big, his protruding belly greatly emphasized by jeans worn too tight. His balding head was covered by a cowboy hat and he held a lit cigar in one hand and a lead rope in another. The rope was attached to the halter worn by one of his Arabian mares. His son James stood on the other side of the horse.

"Frank," the man said in acknowledgement as they got out of the truck.

"How're you doing, Ed?" asked Frank.

"Not so good, I'm afraid," he replied.

"I guess that's why you asked us up here," said Frank.

"Just you, not the adopted son, that's who was asked," smarted James. He chewed on the wad of tobacco in his mouth, spitting juice at Daniel's feet.

"If you have something to say to us, Ed, then you'd better do it. Otherwise, we're going to leave," Frank said.

"It seems one of your wild stallions feels the need to lure some of my mares into his harem," drawled Ed.

"Not possible," replied Frank.

"I beg to differ," the man huffed. "And I can prove it."

"Ed, all of the fencing is intact and working. All of the horses are accounted for. I found every band we have and there are no new horses and none are missing. It's not a horse of ours," Frank said.

"I heard there's one band you can't get close to. How do you know they're accounted for?" interrupted James.

"They're accounted for," Daniel said quietly.

"Prove it," James said.

"Look, we don't have to prove anything. You can take our word or not. There are plenty of other people around here who have horses," Frank said.

"Well, I have a missing mare and this one has these marks on her flanks. You tell me what that is," Ed said, fuming.

"It could be a number of things," Frank replied, looking closely at the marks. "It could be bite marks from another horse or worse, it could be a mountain lion getting too close. We all should be on the look out for that. "

"Well, I think it's that grand stallion you all have from that band that stays up in the trees," James drawled. "He's trying to get more pretty mares to join him."

"You spend a lot of time watching that band through binoculars, don't you?" Daniel asked.

That made James' face turn bright red. "You think you can just come in here and take over everything, don't you? Not even born here and waltz in like you own the place."

"All right, that's enough. We're finished here, Ed," Frank said, motioning Daniel to leave.

"All it takes is one phone call to the BLM, Frank. Say you can't control the horses you have and they can shut you down," Ed shouted.

"Or better yet, they'll ship that stallion off to the slaughterhouse or put a bullet in its head," yelled James, laughing.

Frank turned around and made his way back to the two men. "I'll take that as a threat, Ed. If any of my horses end up missing or dead, I'll report the both of you. I can't stop you from reporting me. But you have to have something to report. Proof. And you don't have it. Hell, you have a stallion here on your own ranch. Could be yours for all we know."

Ed laughed. "Oh, now, Frank, don't get so worked up. How's that beautiful wife of yours doing by the way? Must be nice to have something like that to come home to every night."

"You son of a bitch," Frank began, pointing his finger in Ed's face, but Daniel stopped him.

"We're going now," Daniel said, stepping in front of Frank.

The two of them returned to the truck but it was Daniel who guided Frank to the passenger's side. Frank simply handed the keys to Daniel and got inside. He sat numbly while Daniel drove. He knew he was close to decking the pompous man and also knew that's what Ed had wanted. He had Daniel to thank for preventing it.

"It seems I don't follow my own advice," he said.

"What do you mean?" asked Daniel.

"I told you to not let what James said get to you. But I did just the opposite back there," Frank replied.

"That's all right," said Daniel.

"No, it isn't. I'm not proud of it," Frank said.

"He crossed the line about Sarah. You stood up to him for that," Daniel said.

"I almost did more than stand up to him. Thanks for breaking up something that could've gotten me arrested for assault," said Frank.

"No problem. Rocky," smiled Daniel.

"Rocky?" asked Frank, turning to Daniel.

"Yeah, you know, the fighter," he replied.

"Yeah, I know. Rocky, huh?" he asked, rubbing his chin. "Wonder if I look like him."

"A little grayer, but you could always dye your hair," laughed Daniel.

"That'll be the day," smiled Frank. Daniel probably asked to go with him anticipating trouble somehow and he'd certainly prevented it. Frank looked at the young man sitting next to him with the pride and love a father would have for his son. He'd talk to Sarah about a legal adoption. After what they had experienced, he didn't want any questions in the future about whether or not Daniel deserved something.

"We need to find out if there have been any mountain lion sightings. Keep a lookout ourselves, too," Frank said.

"Okay. Then you think the Tates will let it go now?" Daniel asked.

"No, I don't. It worries me, actually," Frank replied.

"How? Involving the BLM?" asked Daniel.

"Yes, and I wouldn't put it past them to shoot our horses," he said.

"Why? What good would come of that?" Daniel asked, sharply. "I know James threatened, but I guess I didn't think they'd actually do it." He began to worry.

"No good would come of it, but that's not what the Tates are about. They'd do it in a heartbeat if they thought it would drive us away. They want the land. Period," Frank emphasized.

"But they've always wanted the land. This just seems more aggressive than usual," Daniel said.

"I guess they figure you fit in the picture somehow so they're getting desperate," Frank replied.

"Me?" he asked.

"Yes. Sarah and I have talked about this some but I need to discuss it with her about making it legal. We'd like to adopt you, Daniel," Frank replied.

"I don't know what to say," he whispered, tears welling in his eyes.

"Well, I hope you say you'd like to be part of our family. I know you don't need us since you're eighteen, but we feel it would be right," Frank said.

"Yes," he replied simply. Nodding, he pulled the truck to a stop in front of the house and parked. He bowed his head and covered his eyes with his hand, trying to keep the tears from spilling.

"You okay?" Frank asked quietly.

"I am," he began, "and thank you."

"No need to thank us, Daniel. It would be an honor for us," Frank said.

Daniel could only nod again. Words weren't forming and he was too overcome with emotion. He'd never felt wanted in his life until he moved to the ranch. Now he could have a permanent home.

"Well, we'd better check on Cyan and see if everything's set for the sale. If we're lucky, there'll be no hitches," Frank said, patting Daniel on the shoulders.

Daniel followed Frank to the barn. Something he had wished for all of his life had just happened. He would be part of a loving family. It didn't matter that he would soon be turning nineteen. He would have a real family.

———

"I'm sorry, Mrs. Carpenter, false alarm," said the nurse.

"Oh, that's all right. I've had a few of those," Sarah replied.

The nurse looked at her with pity. She had seen it so many times over the years that she'd become immune to it. That look of "poor woman, there must be something wrong with her" masked every face that either conveyed the message she wasn't pregnant or consoled her immediately following a miscarriage. Today was different. She didn't want to wrap herself in the veil of sorrow anymore. She felt relief.

The doctor came into the examining room once she had finished dressing. He had been there from the beginning, through all of the disappointments. It was his advice to never try for children again, so he wasn't as sympathetic as the nurse.

"I have to say I'm surprised," he began.

"I am, too. It wasn't planned. I mean we're not trying to get pregnant," she said.

"Then why would you think you were?" he asked.

"I've not used my diaphragm a couple of times," she said, embarrassed. "But I'm so close to menopause and my periods aren't regular anyway, but it's been a couple of months. I just never thought there'd be a chance after everything we've been through."

"At this point in your life, there's always a chance. Given your history and health," he looked at her with emphasis, "you have to be diligent."

"I know. And I will be from now on," she replied. Upon arriving at the doctor's office, she noticed her cycle had started. The doctor still suggested an ultrasound and pregnancy test to make sure all was normal. It was and she wasn't pregnant.

She left the office with a different state of mind than any of the other times she'd departed. Today she was thankful. In the past she had been brokenhearted. So desolate and inconsolable had she been that she wondered how Frank had managed. Often, weeks would pass before the cloud of despair left her.

Her poor husband. He had been hurting, too, yet all of the focus had been on her loss and how important it was for her to be comforted. He had suffered the losses just as much as she, yet he did so quietly. He was too busy taking care of her. Her heart ached for him.

She couldn't explain her contentment with what had just happened. Maybe she had just reached the point of acceptance and didn't want the heartache ever again. She had Frank in her life and he loved her regardless of the absence of children. Now they had Daniel, not the newborn she had desired, but a teenage boy who had turned into a young man in such a short time. She and Frank loved him like their own son. Perhaps his arrival in their lives brought everything full circle. He was the child they'd always wanted.

It wouldn't be pleasant sharing today with Frank. Her first meeting had been satisfying and she was certain something positive for the equine therapy program would come of it. Frank would be happy for her. He wouldn't be happy about the rest of the day. She couldn't say that she would blame him.

CHAPTER FIVE

"Damn it to hell, Sarah," Frank fumed, "damn it to hell." He stood looking out their bedroom window, his back to her.

She knew he was angry. He had every right to be. She had been careless and telling him so wasn't easy. The look on his face nearly broke her heart. Fear and relief were written there, the same feelings she had experienced earlier. But he had been more afraid of losing her and told her so. She watched him as he stood tall, hands at his waist. The dark in his hair not as prevalent as the gray it was blended with. She also knew he was crying. He never wanted her to see him when he did. She'd never loved him more than she did then.

"I didn't want to be pregnant," she said, putting her face in her hands. She was sitting on their bed, her elbows resting on her legs.

Frank turned to look at his wife, his eyes bright. He saw her small form and he felt like a jerk. She surprised him with that comment. He'd just assumed she would never lose that desire to have their child. How strange to hear her say something he never thought she'd feel. It provided some relief to know she would never intentionally put her life in danger trying to get pregnant, something he immediately thought she had done. He walked to the bed and sat next to her, enveloping her in his arms.

"I'm sorry," he said.

"Me, too," she replied.

They sat like that for a long time, discussing their future. He shared his thoughts on adopting Daniel as soon as possible and she agreed. Legally, he was an adult, so there shouldn't be any issues with the biological father, who no one had heard from in the last three years. Charley had kept them informed, saying the man had become a recluse, stepping out only to buy more booze. He didn't know how he supported himself.

"I'm afraid of what the Tates will do, Frank," Sarah said.

"I know what you mean. They're up to no good and it makes me uneasy," he replied.

"He didn't seem so unkind before his wife died," Sarah said. "I mean he was never pleasant, but now he just seems to have a vindictive side."

"He's always been trouble, but maybe his wife calmed him down a bit. I tell you that son of his is just like him, if not worse," said Frank.

"I've heard he's cruel to his own horses, works them nearly to death," she said.

"It wouldn't surprise me if the son was behind much of Ed's complaint. Plus, the way he acted toward Daniel made my blood boil," he said.

"Well, Daniel has been able to handle himself pretty well," said Sarah.

"If he hadn't been there with me, I might be in jail now," he smiled at his wife.

"Jailbird," she murmured.

"What's this with nicknames? I've collected a few lately," he chuckled.

"Just endearments," she said.

"I guess so," he said.

They decided it was wise to talk to someone with the BLM before the Tates did. Frank knew a fellow there who'd experienced the wrath of Ed Tate a few years ago. Maybe he could help them figure out what to do. It certainly couldn't hurt and it beat sitting around waiting for something to happen.

Daniel had conquered Misfit. The horse had been a challenge but Daniel knew he could do it. He sat astride the horse, riding in a slow trot around the pen. The only issue was when he'd tightened the cinch strap on the saddle. Misfit hadn't cared for that too much. He turned around and bit Daniel on the elbow, while kicking out at the same time. Daniel winced in pain but he didn't get angry. He never got angry, issuing a stern "NO" and pushing the horse's head away. Some people slapped their horses when they misbehaved. It was something he couldn't do, preferring instead to talk. Letting the animal hear your voice calms them and allows them to know you. At least that was his philosophy and it seemed to work for him.

Bob watched him from the shade tree. The dog had been his constant companion from the moment he'd picked the pup up from the shelter, going almost everywhere Daniel went. Shortly after he arrived at the ranch, the only thing he asked for was a dog. The next day, Frank and Sarah took him to the local animal shelter. Daniel knew as soon as he saw the puppy he was the one. Bob was tiny but older than he looked. A retriever mix, his soft brown eyes and coat called out to Daniel and it warmed his heart. The puppy went home with them that day and slept in Daniel's room from that moment on.

Training Bob had been easy. A quick learner and ready to please, the dog had been no problem at all. Daniel's only fear had been the horses. If Bob ventured behind one of them, he could get kicked. So Daniel had to tether Bob more than he liked but it was always where Bob could be close enough to see Daniel. No way would he let Bob get close to Misfit, so the dog enjoyed the shade while being restrained on a long line.

"How're we doing, Bob?" Daniel called to the dog.

The dog looked up, wagging his tail. He let out a single bark in response. Daniel laughed. He was trying to get Misfit used to the sound. So far, so good. The horse didn't react to the bark. He kept trotting at an even pace, Daniel moving in rhythm on the saddle.

Daniel had hung flags and plastic bags around the pen, as part of desensitizing the animal. Horses could get spooked by something as simple as a plastic bag blowing in the wind. Misfit hadn't reacted to any of the distractions. The horse was cued in to Daniel's commands and was following every one of them. His groundwork with Misfit was paying off.

It took him longer with Misfit than any of the other horses, however. Of course, the wild Mustangs didn't count because they were never domesticated. But Misfit at one time had been wild. The horse just didn't know what he wanted to be now. Daniel sensed the animal could probably fly if he'd let him because keeping him at a slow pace was a challenge. Eventually he would see how fast the horse could go, but for now it was about control.

"Whoa," Daniel said, pulling the reins as the horse stopped smoothly. "Good boy."

Daniel patted the horse's neck. He looked like a Paint horse. His broken colored coat had tobiano markings; his flanks, chest and neck were dark brown while much of his face, back and most of his legs were white. Specks of brown dotted the white, with the tail and mane intermixing the two colors but being predominantly white. He was tall and regal, standing about 15 hands. Misfit reminded Daniel of something out of the old west, proud and defiant, a horse that belonged with the Indians riding the plains and defending the land.

"You're a handsome one, Misfit," Daniel said. The horse gently snorted, nodding his head as if in agreement.

"That's right, you know it," Daniel laughed. Looking up, he saw Maria and Joe walking toward the pen. Maria had started coming over in the afternoons with her cousin, driving Joe when he got out of school. Daniel's heart fluttered at the sight of her.

"Well, you did it," she said, smiling, nodding toward Misfit.

"It's a start, at least," he said.

"It's a miracle," Joe said. "If there'd been any horse that would give you trouble, I would've said that one."

"Well, it hasn't been easy. A bite, some bucking and a few kicks later, here we are," replied Daniel.

"And he hasn't thrown you?" asked Joe.

"Not yet. But it wouldn't surprise me if he does. Hope not," shrugged Daniel.

"How can you be so calm about it? Like it's inevitable and okay if it happens," Joe said.

Daniel knew that was Joe's fear talking. He was remembering his own injury and Daniel wasn't sure how to reply. Maria did for him.

"It's okay to be who you are, Joe. I know I couldn't do what Daniel's doing," she said.

"Yeah, but you ride, though," Joe replied.

"Yes, but I didn't go through what you did. Maybe someday you'll want to ride again. If not, that's okay," she said.

Joe shrugged and didn't respond. Daniel exchanged looks with Maria. He sensed something was bothering his friend, something more than his refusal to get back on a horse and the reason behind it.

"James Tate is a jackass," Joe blurted.

"That's nothing new," Daniel replied, getting off of Misfit. He walked the horse over to where Joe and Maria stood.

"It's like he's waiting for me everyday after school, just to torment me," said Joe.

"He's my age. Why is he at the school?" asked Daniel.

"Beats me. But he's there near the buses in his fancy truck, saying crap," said Joe.

Daniel knew there wasn't a high school on the reservation so all of the rez kids went to the public school he'd gone to. They were bused to and from the school and many endured harassment from the moment they stepped through the doors. Some of the white kids made it a point to never extend the welcome mat. James Tate had been one of them. But they had graduated last year. He wondered why James was still hanging out at the school.

"I need to untack Misfit. Follow me," Daniel said. The horse was getting restless and he needed to brush him down. They went to the barn and Daniel removed the bridle, replacing it with a harness so he could use the cross ties. He worked while they talked, unsaddling and brushing.

"From everything I've heard, I hope I never meet the guy," Maria said, referring to James.

"I hope you don't either, but chances are you will," Daniel said.

"He already knows who you are," Joe said dully to her.

"How?' she asked.

"No idea, but he does," replied Joe, looking away.

"Did something happen, Joe?" asked Daniel. For some reason the thought of James Tate knowing Maria didn't sit too well with him.

"Maybe he said some not so nice things and maybe I did some not so nice things to his truck. Or maybe not," Joe said, a sparkle appearing in his eyes.

"What kind of things?" Daniel asked.

"Oh, I don't know. Spray paint might've been involved," Joe replied.

"Joey! That's vandalism. You could get into serious trouble," said Maria.

"No one saw anything. He doesn't even know yet," said Joe.

"Well, he will eventually. Then you'd better watch your back," said Daniel.

"I already have to watch my back with him. Might as well give him a reason," drawled Joe.

"Seriously, if he threatens you at all, I want to know about it," Daniel said.

"Nothing to worry about, right Bob?" Joe said turning to the dog. Daniel had untied the animal, allowing him to follow. Bob sat at Joe's feet, looking up at him and cocking his head sideways as if trying to understand.

"Listen to me, Joe. James Tate is spiteful. He could hurt you and think nothing of it," said Daniel.

"Daniel's right, Joe. Please be careful," Maria said.

"All right, I'll let you know if he says anything," Joe said, giving in.

"Thank you," Daniel replied. He knew Joe wasn't sharing the whole story. Something happened to make him so upset that he resorted to vandalism. Joe was an easy-going guy and took life as it came. Very little riled him.

"C'mon, boy," Daniel said to Misfit, "I've got some sweet hay waiting for you." He guided the horse to one of the stalls and could barely unhook the lead before the horse was chomping for the hay on the floor.

"You act as if you're starving," he said to the horse.

"Horses sure eat a lot," Joe said, coming up behind Daniel. Misfit looked up at them, hay hanging from his mouth, as if to ask, "So?" They both laughed and the horse continued to chew.

"What exactly did Tate say about Maria?" whispered Daniel, looking to see that she wasn't within hearing distance. Maria hadn't followed them and he saw she was sweeping.

"He said to tell you to watch out for your pretty little girlfriend," Joe said, reluctantly. "He really doesn't like you, Daniel."

"Watch out how?" asked Daniel quietly.

"I don't know," Joe said, looking at the floor.

"Tell me," Daniel said, turning to his friend.

"He said some pretty racist things about us, Daniel. Said he might "try her out" if you thought she was so great," Joe said, embarrassed. "His words, not mine."

Daniel felt his blood turn cold and the hairs on his arms stood up. Anxiety, anger and rage were simmering inside him. His head pounded. He feared becoming a monster because thoughts of pummeling James Tate bloody grew. Daniel remembered his father then, the devil, and he thought he was going to throw up.

"Well, say something," Joe said, afraid of the look on Daniel's face.

"I need some air," Daniel said, turning away. He started to head outside but Maria stopped him.

"Are you okay?" she asked, putting her hand on his arm.

"I will be," he replied, kissing her forehead. He searched her face, "Stay with Joe."

As soon as Daniel got outside, he ran. He barely got past any of the buildings before he dropped to his knees and vomited. When his stomach was empty he got up and ran some more. He didn't know where he was going but he needed the air to clear his head. It was the same with the nightmares. They hadn't been as frequent lately but the outcome never changed. He needed a jolt back to reality and something that would calm his nerves.

He reached the top of a small hill and looked down the other side. The expanse was vast. He saw one of the smaller bands of horses grazing near a cluster of trees. No care in the world, Daniel thought, as he looked at them. Listening closely, he could hear them nickering, their way of communicating with each other.

Daniel drank it in, the sights and the sounds. Then he closed his eyes and let his mind drift. He thought of Frank and Sarah and of becoming their son. His mind turned to Maria and the way she turned him to jello. His new life was here with family and friends he reminded himself, with the horses. Not in the dark place he called home three years ago.

"Daniel?" the voice called, full of concern.

He turned to see Frank standing a few feet away. Worry written on his face, he stared at Daniel hoping for an explanation. "Joe found me after you left. Thought something was wrong," he said.

"You know what I'm afraid of?" Daniel began, tears rising, "that I'll become like him. I couldn't take that." Then his shoulders began to shake and he lowered his head, overcome with emotion.

Frank knew he was referring to his father and wondered just how long it would take the scars to heal. Without thinking, he instinctively walked to Daniel, embracing the young man who would become his son. Whatever it took to make him whole again, Frank was willing to try. He and Sarah had talked about encouraging Daniel to try counseling. Maybe it was time to mention it.

"I've known you for over three years now," Frank began after Daniel's tears had subsided, "I've seen nothing but goodness in you."

Daniel didn't respond. "Sometimes talking to someone helps. Someone other than family or friends," continued Frank.

"You mean a shrink?" asked Daniel.

"I mean a counselor," corrected Frank. "Sarah convinced me it might not be such a bad idea. But it's up to you."

"I guess it couldn't hurt," Daniel said.

"Good. Test it out, maybe it'll help," he replied.

"Did Joe mention what set me off?" Daniel asked.

"Well, kind of. Something about James Tate and what he'd said about Maria," Frank replied.

"That's about it," he said.

"Look, I'll give you the same advice I did the other day. The Tates goad people. They want to see a reaction. Ignore it," Frank said. "Most important though, don't take the law into your own hands."

"I saw red. I don't know what I'd do if he ever laid a hand on her," Daniel said.

"Nothing, that's what you do, at least to him. Be there for her. Let the authorities take care of it," he replied. "And Daniel, do a better job of following my advice than I do. Someone might not be there to intervene for you."

Daniel nodded. He knew it was easier said than done but he also knew Frank was right. Reacting the way James Tate wanted was stooping to his level. Plus, he didn't want to see the inside of a jail cell. He was better than that.

"I guess Maria and Joe left," mused Daniel.

"Not sure. That Joe is excitable, though," said Frank.

"What do you mean?" Daniel asked, smiling at Frank's expression.

"He was flappin' and cluckin' like an old hen. It was harder than heck trying to understand what he was saying to me," Frank drawled.

"Sorry about that," laughed Daniel.

"Nothing to be sorry about. He was just worried about you," he said.

"Well, I'm glad he found you," said Daniel.

"Me too. So, how about we get back to the house? Sarah was making those fajitas you like so well," said Frank.

"Definitely," said Daniel, "food always works for me."

"Especially Sarah's. You know, she's the best cook in New Mexico. Heck, probably the whole southwest," Frank said, as they made their way to the truck. Daniel was surprised when he saw it as he'd been so wrapped in thought that he hadn't heard it. Yet, he knew Frank couldn't have gotten there so quickly otherwise.

"I think she's the best cook anywhere. I've never tasted food like hers before," smiled Daniel, sliding in the truck.

"Ha, that'll give her a big head. Think you're right, though," Frank said, winking.

They drove back to the house. Daniel told Frank about Misfit and how easy it had been to ride him, but he knew there was still a lot of work to do with the horse. He laughed at Frank's jokes and he felt relaxed and calm. Once again, he marveled at how lucky he was. Yes, he did think fate had intervened in his case.

CHAPTER SIX

Frank sat in the cramped office facing a small desk that was covered with piles of paper. The cinder block walls were bare, painted pale blue and provided no windows. A small fan stationed on a file cabinet provided the only air and sound in the room. Frank thought he'd go stir-crazy being cooped up like this everyday.

"Hey, Frank, sorry to keep you waiting."

Walter Wright strode into the room and had to squeeze his frame between Frank's chair and the wall to get behind his desk. He looked too big for the office. A former college football player, he studied forestry and found work at the Bureau of Land Management. He'd been with the organization since graduation.

"Good to see you, Walt. Thanks for seeing me on such short notice," Frank said.

"No problem. What can I do for you?" he asked.

Frank told Walt about Ed Tate's complaint and the confrontation he'd had with the man. Walt listened with an impassive expression, pushing the eyeglasses up on the bridge of his nose more out of a nervous habit than need. When Frank finished, the buzz of the fan seemed enormous before Walt spoke.

"You know that Ed Tate hates me, right?" he asked.

"Well, I didn't know the feeling was that strong, but I'd heard there was some conflict a while back," Frank said.

"At one time Ed wanted to adopt some of the wild mustangs we were auctioning," Walt said.

"I had no idea," Frank said.

"I blocked him from being able to. Just something about it didn't smell right," Walt said. "Then he expressed interest in Pryor Mountain and I made the appropriate calls, pulled some strings, saying he didn't have the land, etc. It prevented him from being considered."

"I bet that made his day," drawled Frank.

"He was livid. Came storming in here, making all kinds of threats. Said he'd get me fired," said Walt.

"Luckily, he didn't," commented Frank.

"He tried. It was when I suggested an investigation in to his reasons for wanting the horses that he backed off," Walt said.

"What did you find out?" Frank asked.

"Only that he had no long term plans to keep them once he got them," Walt said. "Rumor has it that he works his horses too much and he once got some mustangs from the reservation. They didn't work to his liking and he sold the horses to some international kill buyers."

"My God," Frank breathed.

"I should add that there was one horse he was very interested in getting and keeping," Walt said. "You own him now."

"Which one?" Frank asked.

"That big dun colored stallion from Pryor Mountain, with the stripe," Walt said.

Espíritu, Frank thought. Daniel's horse. "Ed's son made some crack about that horse to us," he said. "Even accused it of being the culprit."

"You think it's possible?" Walt asked.

"Not a chance," Frank said.

"Well, it sounds like he's holding a grudge now, targeting that horse to get back at you," said Walt.

"Why was he so interested in that stallion?" Frank asked.

"I heard Ed had some grand idea of breeding him. He is a fine looking horse, if I recall," Walt said.

"Yes, he is. But he's wild and reclusive. His herd hasn't had anything to do with anyone since he came to the sanctuary. Daniel's gotten close to him a couple of times but that's it," Frank said. "Ed would've had a helluva time trying to break him."

"Well, you know Ed. Any means necessary," hinted Walt.

"So I've heard," replied Frank.

"Look, I'll keep my ears open and talk to a few folks. You're good to your horses, Frank, so you don't have anything to worry about from our end," Walt reassured him.

"I appreciate that, Walt, but it's Ed I'm worried about," he said.

"Well, we can't do anything at this point, unfortunately. But you brought it to our attention. That's a start," said Walt.

Frank thanked him for his time. Driving home, he knew he'd done the right thing talking to Walt. He'd had some trepidation at first, but needed someone on his side. Walt was a good man.

———

He couldn't have planned it better himself, James Tate thought, chuckling. The whole thing just fell in his lap, like a gift from the heavens. How could he refuse to go along with it? Besides, if it brought pain to Daniel, all the better.

It was impulsive of him to sell his daddy's mare, and probably stupid in the long run, but he needed the money. The two thousand dollars he got for it wasn't nearly what it was worth but the money had helped pay off the debt he owed for his nasty little habit. He'd promised himself he was going to stop the gambling. No more betting, he said each time he did it. But he kept coming back. He couldn't help it. Someday he'd hit the jackpot, he was sure of it. Then he could go to California, putting distance between him and his father's stupid idea of him taking over the business. James had never cared for four-legged beasts anyway and certainly didn't want to follow his father's stupid plan for horse breeding.

How lucky for him that his daddy hated Frank Carpenter just as much as he hated Daniel. Old Ed Tate wanted to believe it was Frank's horses that got the mare he'd sold. So James let him. It certainly took the suspicion off James, plus he still hadn't come up with a way of explaining the horse's absence. Now he wouldn't have to. It was beautiful.

He wasn't sure how the bite marks got on the other mare, however. Probably the fault of their own stupid stallion, just as Carpenter suggested. That horse was a pain in the butt, knocking James down whenever it got the chance. But if his daddy wanted to place the blame on Carpenter's stallion, so be it. He knew his father had wanted that horse something fierce and it stuck in the man's craw that he couldn't get it. It was only worse because Frank had it on the other side of his property line, just enough for his daddy to get a whiff whenever the mood set to him.

James didn't know why he hated Daniel so much. He just did. Daniel had suddenly appeared and everything seemed easy for him. Granted, he was a little quiet and to himself so he wasn't showy like a lot of other people. But that kind of made it worse. He didn't need to brag and blow for people, especially teachers and girls, to notice him. It also didn't help that he was the designated son of his daddy's arch rival, living on the richest ranchland in the area. Daniel didn't deserve it. He wasn't from there. James' blood simmered.

He knew horses meant the world to Daniel. It showed in the way he handled them. James didn't care for them one way or another. So if his daddy saw to it that the Bureau put a bullet in one of the sanctuary's horses, it was fine with him. He'd gladly watch perfect Daniel suffer, while it got him off the hook for the missing mare.

It was only temporary, he knew. The gambling bug made him itch and he couldn't think beyond the present. He'd figure out the next problem when he needed to. What was staring him in the face at the moment was taking care of that little Indian punk that spray-painted his truck. He didn't see it happen but knew who did it. Insulting the kid's pretty little cousin made the boy go over the edge a little bit, smiled James. He'd seen it in his face. And once again, Daniel had the attention of another attractive female. This time, though, Daniel showed interest in return.

James didn't like going near the high school on such a regular basis. People might start to question it, but it was the only place his gambling contact would meet him. Harrassing the kid Joe had just seemed the natural thing to do. James thought it funny how the Indian kid and his cousin connect to Daniel. No wonder he wanted to cause them all pain.

Maybe he should do some digging into Daniel's past. No one had ever questioned why he showed up like he did. Everyone just accepted it. Surely there must be a reason. He'd never heard Daniel talk of family, but then he hadn't been very close to him anyway to know one way or another.

James' new idea put him in a better mood. The potential of finding dirt on Daniel made him smile. He didn't know what he would do with it, but any information that made the golden boy less perfect made James determined to find it, or create it if he had to.

Thinking it was just a matter of time until he could watch Daniel wallow and squirm, James whistled as he jumped up on the tractor. His daddy was short-handed today and needed him to pick up some chores. He'd do so while plotting his little revenge.

CHAPTER SEVEN

"You mean there's actually something you aren't good at?" asked Joe.

"There's a lot I'm not good at," replied Daniel.

"Name something. Other than that thing you don't want to talk about," Joe said.

"Sewing. I don't know how to sew," Daniel said, impatiently.

"That doesn't count. I don't know any guy who knows how to sew," replied Joe.

"Well, there are some. But I'm not one of them," said Daniel.

"I thought all cowboys knew how to shoot a gun," Joe said, changing the subject.

"I'm not a cowboy," replied Daniel.

"And you don't know how to shoot a gun either," Joe said sarcastically.

"Joe, you're trying my patience," said Daniel.

"Nah, I'm not. You're one of the most patient people I know," replied Joe. "Except with a gun."

"Just my luck. You had to be there," Daniel said.

"It was one of the funniest things I've ever seen in my life," laughed Joe.

"I'm glad you got a laugh," Daniel said.

"The way poor Frank hit the ground, I thought you'd shot him," said Joe.

"Yeah, I don't know why he did that," said Daniel.

"He said he was dodging bullets," laughed Joe.

"I know he was just joking around," Daniel said.

"I don't think so. You should've seen the look on his face," Joe replied, laughing harder.

Daniel glanced at Joe and shook his head, smiling. Frank had been trying to get Daniel to shoot for a long time. It just never appealed to him. He had never picked up a gun in his life and didn't want to, although he knew living on a ranch might require it some-day. Driving around at night the way he did without a gun wasn't very wise. He had been lucky. Wild animals roam the land and there might be an occasion when a gun was necessary to protect himself or the horses. So he finally gave in to Frank's suggestion to shoot. It hadn't gone very well.

"I mean how hard is it to hit a coffee can?" Joe asked loudly, bring-ing Daniel back to the embarrassing situation.

"Pretty hard, actually," Daniel said.

"It was when Frank said to keep your eyes open that I thought maybe I should leave," said Joe, teasing.

"Maybe you should have," muttered Daniel.

"Not a chance. I couldn't miss out on seeing the action, even if it meant getting hit by a ricocheting bullet," he said.

"Well, you didn't. So give it a rest," replied Daniel.

Daniel knew Frank was disappointed but at the same time thought the whole situation pretty funny. He saw how hard it had been for Frank to suppress laughter at a few of his wild misses, particularly when Joe provided the colorful commentary.

He didn't know Frank could move so fast. Daniel smiled. Quick as lightning would be a better way to describe it and he guessed he'd be dodging bullets, too, if he'd been in Frank's shoes. He appreciated Frank's encouragement, though. Not once did he make light of the fact Daniel simply couldn't shoot. Daniel was determined to learn. He might never be the best shot in the world, but he would learn to shoot.

"Maybe you could try archery," said Joe, interrupting his thoughts.

"What? And carry a bow and arrow around in the truck?" Daniel asked.

"Why not? Or you could strap it on your back when you're riding. You know my ancestors did it," reminded Joe.

"Well, why don't I just carry a tomahawk then?" asked Daniel.

"That's an idea. But all require the ability to aim, so that might be out of the question," said Joe.

"Very funny. Don't you have somewhere you need to be?" Daniel asked.

"I never have to be anywhere. Aren't you lucky?" teased Joe.

"Well, then help me straighten up the tack room," Daniel said, handing Joe a saddle pad that hadn't been returned to the proper shelf after use.

They worked, with Daniel instructing Joe as to where things should be placed. Neither mentioned the gun lesson again that day.

———

"It's just over there," Bill said.

Frank got out of the truck and followed Bill. The two men routinely patrolled the property line, ensuring the fencing was secure. But since the threat by the Tates, they had doubled the time checking, with Daniel patrolling as well. The fencing was always intact, but what Bill had just found made Frank angry.

"Yep, you're right," he said. "Barbed wire. Tossed right over the fence. I'll be damned."

"I just hope none of the horses have come in contact with it," Bill murmured.

"Me, too," he sighed. "I don't see any blood anywhere and it doesn't look as if it's been dragged, so we probably just found it. I worry that there's more somewhere on the property, though."

Frank knew that if a horse got tangled up in barbed wire, it could be the kiss of death for the animal. It could mangle itself so badly trying to get loose, that the wounds would never heal. Putting it down would be the only alternative.

"We have a lot of patrolling to do, I guess," Frank said. "Thing is, we could cover every inch of this place and still miss it." He pushed the brim of his hat back on his brow and wiped his forehead.

"And we could patrol today, and they leave the wire tomorrow," Bill said, shaking his head.

"I don't have enough manpower. This is too big of a job for the three of us, not to mention the hay fields, horses and everything else that needs tending to. I don't have men to spare," Frank said.

"I might be able to get you some help," Bill said. "I know a few guys looking for some part time work. I'll talk to Merrill, too. Get him to ask around."

"I'd appreciate it. As long as they don't bother the horses, we'll take any help we can get," Frank replied.

The two of them picked up the rest of the wire and threw it in the back of Frank's truck. Bill had already put some of the wire in his own truck before radioing Frank about his find. They got lucky in discovering it when they did. Hopefully they'll be just as lucky in that there won't be anymore. Frank was doubtful. And if not barbed wire, what next?

He'd get Daniel to go out with him later. Not only did they have to check for anything dangerous left on the property, they had to routinely check on the herds of horses. It wasn't easy because they couldn't always find every band. On any given day, there were three or four bands you'd likely come across because they were more conditioned to humans. The rest were always hit or miss, since the herds were always on the move.

Then there was Espíritu's band. Frank smiled. Daniel had named the great stallion and it fit perfectly. Ghost or Spirit. The horse kept his harem farthest away so more than likely the only checking up on them would be through binoculars. Although he might suggest coming along with Daniel one night to see if he too could get a closer glimpse.

He hadn't been near the stallion since shortly after they brought the horse to the ranch. Spirited and angry, Espíritu was difficult to contain. His journey from Pryor Mountain to New Mexico hadn't been easy. He had been in some of the herds the BLM rounded up and it was decided he was too old to release back in the wild. Branded, he went up for adoption. There were many who wanted him but most had ideas of training and breeding. Frank knew by looking at the horse they'd never be successful. He was magnificently wild and would fight to the death to stay that way. So Frank was determined to let him live the rest of his life freely, even if it was on sanctuary land.

Espíritu was not confined for long once Frank got him to New Mexico. The veterinarian came to the ranch as soon as they arrived to check out the horse and give him a clean bill of health. Or as well as he could. The stallion wouldn't allow much interaction with anyone, bucking, biting and kicking anything and anyone that got close enough. While frustrating, it was also one of the most thrilling experiences Frank ever had with a wild one. The stallion's spirit was alive and it made Frank proud that he'd started the sanctuary.

Releasing the great beast was one of the most magnificent things he'd ever witnessed. The animal had bolted into the wind, and when far enough away, stopped and turned to look back at them. He stood tall and proud, mane whipping wildly. He stomped his front legs and then bucked, snorting and neighing. It was as if he were telling them all, "this is the way it must be".

When Frank got Espíritu, he also obtained a couple of mares at the same time. All three stayed within the same herd after he brought them home. The mares simply followed the stallion once they were released, as if that was what they were supposed to do. And all three have remained together. There are additions to the band, of course. Some mares Espíritu stole from other bands joined his harem and there have been a few offspring. It was one of the larger herds at the sanctuary.

Frank knew the Tates were behind the wire being tossed on his land. More than likely the son was the instigator. He'd report it to Walt and to the local sheriff's department. There wasn't much more he could do other than patrol the area non-stop until all of the senselessness ended. It was anybody's guess as to when that would be.

His mind wandered to the shooting lesson he'd tried to give Daniel. He wasn't joking when he said he couldn't shoot. He knew

Daniel needed to learn if he continued living on the ranch, but Frank didn't fancy getting shot by a ricocheting bullet. He'd have to come up with a better idea and next time make sure Joe was nowhere to be found. That kid could talk until you wished you were deaf.

He got in his truck and began to drive back to the house. Eventually, they'd need to mow and rake the alfalfa so it could dry out some before it was baled. Along with hoping for no rain during that time, he also wished the whole mess with the Tates would be over. The hay season would take him through September and he needed as many people devoted to that project as possible. He didn't know how he could spare anyone to pull triple duty guarding the horses on the sanctuary, but it had to be done.

Pulling up their drive, he saw Sarah working outside. She was raking and clearing winter debris from the gardens. Her long chestnut hair glistened underneath the hat she wore. He loved brushing her hair, hearing the crackling as the brush eased through the strands, and feeling the softness as it played through his fingers. He always marveled at how little gray she had. He had enough for the both of them, she joked. Frank smiled. His heart always jumped at the sight of her.

Getting out of the truck, he walked up to his wife and put his arms around her. Then he grabbed another rake and started working. Together they cleared and removed the earth's winter coat, revealing new growth breaking through much of the soil. They worked like that, side by side, until the sun dipped on the horizon.

CHAPTER EIGHT

Daniel drove the truck along the road. The sun was beginning to set and the days were getting longer. Temperatures were getting warmer and soon they'd all be baking under the hot southwestern sun. Summer always brought anxiety and worry over the alfalfa hay crops the ranch produced. Timing was everything in when to mow, rake, dry out and bale. Weather forecasts were followed closely because rain was never a good thing when the hay was left to dry. If baled when wet, the hay could grow mold and go bad. An animal that ate bad hay could get sick and sometimes die.

In the years Daniel had been at the ranch, he had never experienced a poor hay crop. But Frank told tales of a couple of summers when the ranch lost the entire crop mainly due to unusual amounts of rain and hail storms. While a large portion of the hay was sold, a good deal of it was used to supplement grazing during the winter months for the sanctuary horses. He realized how important the hay crops were.

Now they had the additional worry of keeping the horses safe. He knew without a doubt that James Tate was behind the barbed wire Frank and Bill found. He wasn't sure about the dad, but his gut told him it was definitely the son. If only they could catch him in the act.

His mind turned to where he was headed. He was almost at Merrill's house where Maria waited for him. They were going out on a date and Daniel was nervous. They'd spent a lot of time together already, just doing things. She had helped him at the ranch and he found himself clearing tables at the Turnout while waiting for her and Joe to finish working. That always brought amusement to Joe's face and something a little harsher to Merrill's. While it wasn't a frown, the man wasn't as welcoming as he used to be. Daniel suspected it was due to his interest in Maria.

She opened the door after his knock and as usual, after each time he saw her, he had trouble forming words that made any sense. It was as if his eyes had to drink in the vision before his brain allowed him to do much more than mumble. And Maria was a beautiful vision.

"Hi, Daniel," she said. Her smile made the outside corners of her eyes crease, emphasizing her cheekbones and the dimple to the right side of her face.

"Did you know that you have a dimple under your right cheekbone when you smile, but not on the other side?" he asked, staring at her face.

"Yes," she laughed, "I did. I hope you don't think I'm flawed or something."

"No. Never," he said, his eyes breaking the trance from her face and looking down at his feet. He shoved his hands in his jeans pockets.

"Do you want to come in?" she asked.

"Sure," he nodded, stepping through the open door.

The living room was furnished sparsely. A chair was in the corner and behind it was a floor lamp illuminating the space. Next to it, against the longest wall stood an oversized sofa and a coffee table was set in front of it. Both the chair and sofa had a worn look, with faded fabric and matching pillows. There was nothing on the walls except for a crucifix at the opposite end of the room. The only other furniture was an old upright piano. A single framed photo set on top of it. Daniel looked closer and saw an image of a man with a small child.

"Is that you and your dad?" he asked.

"Yes," replied Maria, "in happier times."

He looked at her questioningly, expecting her to explain. She put her forefinger to her lips, and glanced over her shoulder. It was a gesture to indicate silence because someone in another room would overhear their conversation. And as if on cue, Merrill loomed in the doorway of the kitchen staring at them. The light at his back made him appear larger and more intimidating than he was, Daniel thought.

"Hello, Daniel," he said.

"Oh, hey, Merrill," Daniel replied.

"Where are you two off to?" the man asked.

"We thought we'd see a movie," Daniel said.

"Papa, I already told you," Maria said with impatience.

"I know, I know," he said, with a little laugh.

"You ready?" Maria asked Daniel.

"Sure," he replied. "I'll see you later, Merrill."

"Bye. Don't be too late," came his reply.

"We won't, Papa," Maria said, closing the door behind them.

"He's become such a worrier lately," she continued, as they got in the truck.

"Well, does it have anything to do with the two of us going out?" he asked.

"I don't know, maybe," she said.

"You do know, don't you?" he asked gently. "It's okay to tell me. It's pretty obvious."

"It isn't you. He likes you a lot. It's because you aren't Navajo," she said.

"Not anything I can do about that," he said.

"I know. And he'll get past it. It isn't as if he's steeped in the cultural ways himself, even though he thinks he should be and has tried living it," she replied.

"How so?" Daniel asked.

"Well, my parents are divorced, and I think it bothers Papa more than it does my mom. I don't think it's something he wanted. Daniel," she looked at him, changing the subject, "do you ever think of going to college?"

"My life has been getting through one day at a time, I guess. Not much planning beyond that until I moved here and got my head straight," he said.

"But do you think about it now?" she asked.

"I've given it thought, yes. I'd like to do something with horses. I guess I should think more seriously about it now that I've been out of high school a year," he replied.

"I'm going in the fall. You should think about it," she said. "I think that's another reason Papa is worried about you."

"He's afraid I'll keep you from going to school?" he asked.

"Yes, I think so," she replied.

"Well, I won't keep you from doing anything that you want to do," he said, smiling at her. "What did you mean back there? In happier times?"

She shrugged. "I don't know. The things I remember about being a family were good times. I remember my parents laughing a lot and we did things together. But suddenly it ended and my mom wanted a divorce."

"Did you ever find out why?" he asked.

"Mom tried explaining it to me when I got older. Said she didn't want to live on the rez anymore. She wanted more opportunity for me. Papa couldn't accept that, I guess," she said.

"But he wants you to go to school," Daniel added.

"Yes, but he also wants me to respect my culture, too. I do that I guess. In my own way, just not the way he'd like," Maria said.

They drove until the lights of town greeted them. A lot of people were strolling the sidewalks and some were window shopping, while others stood around laughing and talking with friends. Friday nights saw the stores staying open later hoping to catch a little more business. The crowd seemed to be taking advantage of the milder temperatures after the cold winter and browsing a bit longer.

Daniel found a parking place near the movie theatre. Taking her hand in his, the two of them walked up to a group of teens waiting in line to buy tickets. One member of the group recognized him.

"Well, well, if it isn't the great Daniel. Come to join the ranks of us normal people, huh?" came the voice of James Tate.

Just hearing him talk made Daniel go on alert. Instinctively, he stepped slightly in front of Maria, shielding her from the other boy's lewd glance.

74

"How's it goin', James?" Daniel asked.

"How's it goin', he asks," James mimics to his companions standing around him. The two male friends laughed nervously, not finding what he had to say funny and smelling trouble with his words. Daniel recognized one of the guys as someone he'd liked back in high school.

Daniel felt Maria pulling at his arm, trying to get him to move away. He knew she sensed the hostility from James. Anyone could. He wanted to leave but they had planned to see the movie. They shouldn't be forced to change their plans because of a bully.

"Well, that pretty little thing hanging on your arm sure is done up right," James laughed, too loudly.

Daniel gritted his teeth, his jaw set in anger. He could feel the heat rising in him, and all it had taken was for James to mention Maria. He remembered Frank's words about goading and not letting James get to him. It took a great deal of will power to calm down. He counted to ten silently.

"What? You can't talk?" James asked loudly.

"Don't have much to say," Daniel began, turning to Maria and said, "c'mon."

They started to move from the line but James wasn't letting up. He stepped as closely as he could, trying to block their way, but something in the way Daniel stared at him caused him to stop. Usually anyone James Tate tried to intimidate either looked down in submission or looked away. But Daniel's eyes didn't waver from James' face. Daniel didn't show fear and suddenly James wondered what would happen if he pushed Daniel too far. A feeling of panic replaced James' confidence and he stepped aside, making a sweeping motion with his arm.

"After you," he said, bowing.

Daniel and Maria moved ahead in the line, walking up to the ticket window. Daniel had no idea what had just happened. It could've escalated into something ugly but hadn't. Whatever reprieve he was getting from this encounter would be short-lived. James Tate had an ax to grind but tonight he'd backed down. There was sure to be another time.

Daniel tried to put it out of his mind. He smiled at Maria as they went into the movie theatre. Her worried eyes had relaxed and the smile she wore reached them. It lit up her face and took Daniel's breath away. James Tate slipped from his consciousness and he wrapped himself in the warmth that was Maria. Nothing else mattered for him that night.

———

"Dammit," swore James. "Dammit, dammit, dammit!"

He punched the steering wheel for emphasis each time he said the word. Not that it mattered. He was the only one sitting in his truck. His so-called friends decided to call it a night. "Jerks," he muttered, thinking of them. They hadn't seemed pleased with him that night, and he got a sense they liked Daniel, for whatever reason. They didn't want to be part of his little game and it pissed him off.

Seeing Daniel had taken James by surprise. The guy rarely left his ranch, so it was sort of a shock when he turned around and found him standing there. And the taunting words just came spilling out of his mouth, especially when he noticed that pretty Maria standing next to him. Saintly Daniel sickened him. Jealousy burned in his gut.

James reached for a beer he had chilling in the cooler on the seat next to him. He wasn't old enough to buy it but always took from his dad's stash. It wasn't like anyone would notice. The housekeeper kept Ed Tate's alcohol supply well stocked. Little did they know, she was buying for the son, too.

He took a sip. It felt good as it touched his tongue. His reaction to Daniel had surprised him. It was the first time in his life that he'd backed down from anything, but something about Daniel's piercing stare made the hair on the back of his neck stand up. He'd suddenly worried what Daniel might be capable of doing to him if he found himself in a fight with the guy.

Daniel was tall and muscular and had a greater physical presence than James. It occurred to him that Daniel could probably beat him to a pulp if he wanted to. James' self-preservation outweighed picking a fight with someone like Daniel. He had to be careful.

Taking another sip, his mind wandered. He knew there were other ways of getting to Daniel. Ways that wouldn't implicate him, at least not directly. He didn't think the good Daniel would bring him any harm if he couldn't prove James guilty of anything. James didn't understand people like that. In his way of thinking, you never got ahead in life if you always gave up your place to everyone else.

He could find a means of getting further onto the sanctuary land but it would be tricky now. Leaving that barbed wire had probably been a mistake as it had alerted all of them to the problem and hadn't done any damage as far as he could tell. He should have just taken a shotgun and killed a few of the horses. Put an end to all of it.

He smiled and drained the can of beer, belching loudly. There was always that pretty little Maria, too. Man would he like to have some fun with her. The thought excited him. But he had to be careful there, too. Daniel would definitely find out about any goings on with her. He'd have to come up with a plan.

Then there was Joe. He owed the kid one anyway for what he'd done to James' truck. It cost him an arm and a leg to get it repainted, putting the expense on his daddy's credit card, something else he'd have to explain to Ed Tate at some point. So James hadn't exacted his revenge yet. But he would.

Tomorrow was the last day of school before summer break and he'd been told he couldn't meet there anymore afterward. Too risky since no kids would be around that they could blend in with. So he'd go over, do his business and then take care of some business with that pest of an Indian. James Tate would show that punk Joe he wasn't one to screw around with. It still didn't solve the problem with Daniel, but he had to do it. It might be the last chance he'd see the kid around for a while.

Smiling, he opened another beer and started the engine. The thought of exacting revenge tomorrow helped ease the frustration he had felt earlier. Daniel was a thorn in his side and James had to figure out a way to remove it.

———

Maria couldn't sleep. The thoughts of Daniel and the evening she'd spent with him wouldn't leave her mind. She liked the way her hand fit in his and the way he acted like a protector even though it wasn't intentional. It was just him. She liked the way his blue eyes turned soft when she caught him staring at her, and the way he smelled, and the way he smiled when he teased her. Pretty much everything about him held her interest and even more. His presence was powerful and intoxicating, like a drug you had no control over. She couldn't get enough of it.

They had kissed before but that night was different. The first kiss led to many more, deeper and longer and more passionate until she could barely stand it. She'd never had sex before but knew she wanted to with Daniel. All she wanted was to be with him. And they would have if Daniel hadn't ended it. His murmurs of "not here" slowly brought her out of the fog of passion and into reality, one that found their half-dressed forms awkwardly entwined on the seat of Daniel's truck.

She knew eventually they would be together. The thought caused a conflict of emotions to swirl in the pit of her stomach. Contentment, impatience, anticipation and longing made her restless. She tried to get her mind on other things.

Her thoughts turned instead to something unpleasant. James Tate's hatred for Daniel was obvious. She'd seen it written in the snarl he wore on his face that night at the movie theatre. He was itching to pick a fight with Daniel and started as soon as he'd laid eyes on them. But just as abruptly, he stopped, as if something had scared him.

The guy gave her the creeps. She saw the way he stared at her. His face told her what he'd like to do to her and it made her uneasy. She knew Daniel saw it, too, and felt him bristle when James mentioned her name. James was looking for trouble any way he could get it and she had to make sure Daniel didn't give it to him, especially if it had anything to do with her.

She closed her eyes, determined to sleep. Even a couple of hours were better than none. Thoughts of Daniel clouded her mind and made her drowsy. Maria allowed herself to drift close to the edge of the precipice, until the need for slumber plunged her over the edge and into darkness. She finally slept.

———

"Holy hell," Daniel mumbled as he tossed restlessly.

He sat up in bed, rubbed his eyes and ran his hands through his hair. It had been one sleepless night. He looked at the alarm clock. Four a.m. He might as well just call it a night and get up for the day.

His thoughts wandered back to that night with Maria. He had no words to describe the softness of her skin. The tiny goose bumps that arose wherever he'd touched or kissed nearly sent him over the edge. They had both almost lost control and stopping was the hardest thing he'd ever done in his life. But as much as he wanted her, he didn't want it to happen that way. Their first time together needed to be special. Call him old-fashioned for the times, but that's who he was.

He wondered if she'd been able to sleep any. Probably not, he smiled, remembering the way she had kissed him, her moans soft against his ear. She was just as frustrated as he had been when they stopped. It was now his mission to find a place for them to be together.

The memory of James Tate's words burned in his mind, however. And it riled Daniel to see the way he looked at Maria. It took great effort to ignore the bully but he did it. He had to remember to use the same self-control in the future with James.

CHAPTER NINE

Frank had needed this morning ride. It soothed his soul to feel the wind in his face as the colors of the sky lightened, announcing a new day. He and Sarah had always loved the mornings, easily rising early, never wanting to waste precious daylight hours. Sarah often joked it was a good thing they weren't night owls since their jobs required them to be early risers.

That morning he had ridden alone, taking his favorite horse Mac along with him. Mac was a chestnut colored Quarter Horse and he had been with Frank for years. In fact, it was Sarah who named him.

"Macbeth," she'd declared upon seeing the colt, "because he stands tall, like a king."

And so the frisky, little Macbeth grew into the strong, dependable beauty called Mac. And the horse loved Frank. There weren't many horses that could be called by name that would immediately come running. But Mac would. All Frank had to do was yell for Mac in his paddock or out in the pasture, and the horse would come trotting to his side, just as a dog would do. Sarah said it was a good thing he hadn't taught the young Mac to sit on Frank's lap, because she could easily see the older Mac trying to do it.

That morning, he had ridden the horse out to the alfalfa fields, checking the progress. The plants looked good and if the weather cooperated, the first cutting should be right on the usual schedule. Frank always worried this time of the year. The alfalfa hay crops weren't do or die for them financially, by any means. But he had a lot of people depending on his hay production, not to mention it fed all of the sanctuary horses through the winter. There was always a lot riding on its success.

He and Mac found their way back to the house by way of one of the many streams that helped irrigate the property. Stopping to allow the horse to drink, Frank marveled at nature's beauty. Chirping birds competed with the sound of rushing water. Sagebrush scented the air and the sky was a blue only found in New Mexico. He had to pinch himself sometimes to remind him how lucky he and Sarah were. How different things could have been.

Reaching the barn, Mac nickered in anticipation, knowing he'd get a treat of mash after he was untacked. "Am I that predictable, old boy?" Frank asked. The horse nuzzled Frank's neck, as if replying yes.

Frank wondered about everyone's mood that weekend. Sarah was distracted with planting and thoughts of the equine therapy program. Daniel had been distant and a little foul-tempered both days, not wanting to talk much. Frank knew something was on his mind. Even Bill appeared agitated about something, only mentioning that he was a little worried about Joe but wouldn't elaborate.

"Must be a full moon, huh?" he asked Mac, as he gently brushed the sweating horse down. Mac stuck his bottom lip out and rested his left back leg, indicating he was fully relaxed and enjoying the feel of the brush against his skin.

The sound of horses neighing brought Mac's ears up. Frank knew the horses had seen Daniel who would be feeding them their morning ration of hay, so they were making their impatience known. He smiled at the image he knew so well. One of the sweetest horses out there was Sarah's gelding, Tuck, a Tennessee Walking Horse. Tuck shared a paddock with a couple of other older geldings. In a separate paddock were Daniel's horse, Sun, a Quarter Horse he took to when he first came to the ranch, along with three other geldings. Misfit was slowly being immersed with the horses and liked to hang around a couple of other horses that belonged to boarders.

Soon Bill would be cleaning the stalls and the three of them would start making their rounds with the sanctuary horses. The fields should be growing enough to allow for grazing now, but they sometimes supplemented with hay if they wished to close off a portion of land to the wild horses, allowing for sufficient healthy growth in the future.

They hadn't found any more barbed wire but continued to be diligent in searching for it. Frank didn't think the Tates had given up their quest for whatever revenge they thought he deserved. He kept his eyes open for anything.

He had alerted Walt at the BLM about their find just for the record. Walt indicated he'd heard some grumblings via the grapevine Ed Tate was making about Frank. He assured Frank that he knew they were baseless allegations and he'd make sure everyone else did, too.

"Good morning," came Sarah's voice, interrupting his thoughts.

"Morning," he replied, turning to see his wife. She was holding a thermos and a basket covered with a dishtowel.

"I noticed you didn't make any coffee for yourself this morning. Thought you might like to join me. I made some fresh muffins, too," she said, indicating the basket.

"That sounds good. Let me finish up here," he said, leading the horse to a stall. Mac's nostrils twitched, as he smelled the muffins Sarah was holding. She laughed.

"None for you, old boy, but I know you'll get some carrots or apple slices to enjoy with that mash," she said.

"Well, I guess I'm more predictable than the weather. Even Mac knew he was getting mash," Frank said, returning to his wife.

"Definitely. And dependable. It's one of the things I love about you," she said, lifting up to kiss his cheek.

He took the thermos and basket from her and set them down on a bench. Putting his arms around his wife, Frank said, "Surely dependability isn't high on the list of my good qualities."

"Right up there with handsome," Sarah replied, kissing him again.

"You know, I probably smell like Mac right now. Not a good idea to get too close," he said, closing his eyes and enjoying the feel of her.

"Are you trying to get rid of me?" she asked, kissing his neck.

"No, just saving you from thinking you're kissing Mac," he replied.

"I like Mac," she said, "but I love you."

"And I love you," he said, kissing her back.

She was intoxicating, Frank thought. The woman made him dizzy, even after all these years together. How did he ever get so lucky? He knew a lot of men his age lived in either loveless marriages or ones where the excitement had waned to simple fondness. Too often those men looked at any woman who might return their glance and even the ones who didn't. And sometimes it went farther than looking.

Frank knew he'd never cheat on Sarah and he had no desire to be with another woman. There had been times in their marriage when a few women who briefly entered their lives came on to him. Two or three offered him blatant invitations. It just never appealed to him. He loved Sarah and couldn't imagine hurting or deceiving her that way. Often, he wondered how those women would feel if they were the ones being cheated on. If they hadn't experienced it, they probably would. That was the sad reality of it.

"Oh, sorry," Daniel said from the back of the barn. "Seems I always interrupt the important stuff."

Frank and Sarah looked at him as they embraced. Daniel was smiling as he stared at the two of them.

"Yeah, you know how to enter at just the right time," Frank teased.

"You want some coffee, Daniel, or some blueberry muffins?" Sarah asked, moving from Frank and picking up the basket.

"Sure. Just a muffin," he replied.

Sarah took two mugs from the basket and poured coffee for Frank and herself. She passed the plate of muffins around and watched Daniel devour two of them with about four bites. He was starting on his third as she was reaching for her first.

"Worked up an appetite this mornin'?" Frank asked with amusement.

Daniel swallowed and said, "I guess I was a little hungry."

"Just a little?" Frank asked.

"There are more in the kitchen, so eat up," Sarah laughed.

"Okay," Daniel said, smiling at Sarah and reaching for another, wiping his mouth with the back of his hand.

Frank exchanged amused glances with Sarah. He saw the twinkle in her eyes. She had told him before that feeding him and Daniel was like cooking for a small army. The two of them could eat more food than she could ever dream of putting away. That wasn't saying much, Frank thought, since she ate like a bird, but he would admit that he enjoyed good food. So did Daniel. Fortunately, that hadn't caught up with either Frank or Daniel's sizes. Daniel had the lean weight of youth and Frank was fortunate that his metabolism hadn't slowed much with age.

"Frank, oh god, Frank," came Bill's frantic cry.

They turned to see Bill standing before them with a dazed face, tears falling freely. He was shaking and in his hand was his cell phone.

"What is it, Bill?" Frank asked.

"Inez," Bill mumbled.

"Did something happen to Inez?" Sarah asked.

"No, no," he began, but couldn't seem to finish.

"Take a deep breath, Bill. Tell us what happened," Frank said.

"Inez, phone," Bill started, handing up his cell phone. Sarah took the phone from him. "Joe's been hurt."

"What happened to Joe?" Daniel asked.

"He's at the hospital, beaten up," Bill cried, "I worried something was going on."

"What do you mean?" asked Frank.

"He's been skittish lately, begging not to go to school, but I made him," Bill cried. "He wouldn't tell me why."

The man was inconsolable, blaming himself for making Joe go to school. Frank saw that Sarah was talking on Bill's cell phone and gathered she was having a conversation with Inez. He glanced at Daniel, who wore a mask of concern mixed with anger.

"Okay, that was Inez," Sarah said, ending the call and placing her hand on Bill's arm. "Everything's going to be fine."

"Where is Joe?" asked Daniel.

"He's in the emergency room, getting a few stitches," she replied hesitantly, looking at Frank.

"I'm going over there," Daniel said, starting to leave.

"Wait," Frank said. "Let's all go together. And I'll drive."

"No, no. I need my truck," Bill said.

"Bill, I'll drive you over in your truck. Frank and Daniel can go in ours. Does that work?" Sarah asked the man. He nodded.

When they reached the hospital, none of them could keep up with Daniel's pace. He nearly ran from the truck and into the building. They followed the signs to the "Emergency Room" and stopped at the front desk.

"I'm sorry, but only next of kin can go back," came the woman's emotionless voice from behind the workstation. The stick of gum she chewed crackled in the silence.

"I'm the father," Bill said, sniffing.

"Through those doors," the woman pointed, "down the hallway and take the first left."

They watched Bill disappear through the "Authorized Personnel Only" entrance. Frank took Sarah's hand and put his other hand on Daniel's shoulder. They stood that way together watching the doors as if waiting for someone to emerge with good news.

"Let's sit down," Frank said, finally.

The room was empty. They sat in three worn out, upholstered chairs closest to the doors. A television, mounted to the wall, provided the only sound.

"So how bad is it really?" Daniel asked Sarah, referring to her phone call with Inez.

"Not bad enough to need a hospital stay," she said, putting her hand on his.

"But bad enough to come here," Daniel mumbled, recalling the times he'd been brought to the ER due to the devil's rages. It had been a long time since his last visit but time didn't dim the pain he'd felt, or the fear.

"Did Inez have any ideas as to what happened?" Frank asked.

"All she said was that it took place this morning at school. When she asked Joe what happened, he didn't want to talk about it," Sarah replied. "No one at the school saw anything, I guess."

"Or they're just not saying," Daniel said, angrily.

"Look, Daniel, we don't know that," Frank began.

"I know that it was James Tate. I also know that it's hard for kids like Joe to be in that school," Daniel said.

"We can't accuse anyone until Joe decides to tell us what happened," Frank said gently.

"What would James Tate be doing at the school?" asked Sarah.

"I don't know, but Joe said he was there a lot, mainly after school," Daniel replied.

"Does this have anything to do with what you told me the other day? Something that James Tate had said about Maria?" Frank asked Daniel.

"Maybe so," Daniel mumbled, "but there could be more to it."

"It's going to be okay," Frank said, patting Daniel on the back. "Let's hear what Joe has to say before we jump to any conclusions."

Daniel nodded. He was itching to get up and go through those doors, authorized personnel or not, and find out for himself. He needed to see Joe and make sure his friend was all right. If Joe pinned Tate for the incident, it would take all of the state of New Mexico to keep him from going after the bastard. That was something he didn't want to do.

The sound of the doors opening caused all three of them to stand and look expectantly. Inez walked through first, her face puffy and eyes downcast. Behind her was Bill, who hovered over the wheelchair that was being pushed beside him. Joe sat patiently in the chair, his face almost unrecognizable. One eye was nearly swollen shut, his nose and mouth were cut and split, stitches marked his cheek and forehead. Shades of purple and green cast faint hues under his eyes and would only deepen as the days passed.

Daniel rushed to the wheelchair and bent down. "Joe, what happened?" he asked.

"Hey, Daniel," Joe muttered, a single tear ran from the "good" eye.

"Who did this?" Daniel asked gently.

"I can't talk so good," came the whispered reply.

"It's okay, it's okay," Daniel reassured him.

"We must go," said Inez, "the Hataali will come."

"Maybe I'll come by tomorrow, just to check on you," Daniel said.

"No, not possible," Bill said. "It could take several days. It's up to the Hataali."

Inez hugged Sarah and the three of them left the building, with Joe being pushed in the chair by a nurse. Frank put his arms around the two most important people in his life and they stood there together until the nurse returned with the empty wheelchair.

"Excuse, me," Frank began to the nurse, "just how bad are his injuries?"

The nurse eyed them, wondering how much to reveal. Finally, she simply said, "No broken bones or internal injuries, but he took a beating. He's actually pretty lucky." She then wheeled the chair through the forbidden doors and was gone.

"Somehow I don't think he feels very lucky," muttered Frank.

"What did they mean back there? Hataali. What's that?" asked Daniel.

"Medicine man," Frank replied.

"They'll have a Navajo healing ceremony for Joe. Outsiders aren't welcome," Sarah added.

"And it could take days, so you have to be patient and ride it out," Frank said, with meaning.

"Yes, we have to follow Inez and Bill's lead on this. It's part of their culture," said Sarah, patting Daniel's arm.

It was two weeks before they saw Bill and Inez. Both returned to work on the same day as if nothing had happened. Eventually they opened up to Frank and Sarah, expressing their frustration that Joe wouldn't name the person or people who had hurt him. They had talked to the rez police and were told that unless Joe was willing to talk, nothing could be done. And since it didn't happen on reservation land, they didn't have any jurisdiction over it anyway. No one at the school claimed to see anything either. So Joe was the only one who could reveal anything and he wasn't willing to do it.

Joe's stubbornness infuriated Daniel. No matter how hard Daniel tried to get him to talk, he refused. It was as if he needed to protect someone by remaining silent. Daniel was certain Joe had been threatened somehow, maybe with further violence to him or his family, if he accused anyone. There was a good chance James Tate was going to get away with what he'd done. Daniel knew it was Tate but he couldn't convince Joe to admit it.

CHAPTER TEN

The devil was back. He was larger than Daniel remembered but his voice was the same. Hissing and spewing ugliness and hatred, the mean glint of his eyes bespoke evil. He was there to tear down everything Daniel had accomplished. Fear gripped Daniel and he wanted to run but there was nowhere to go. The devil had come for him and was ready to do harm. Daniel must escape.

"No," Daniel whimpered.

But the devil just smiled, raising his hand to strike. The blows came, one after the other, but Daniel didn't feel them. Not one. Something was wrong. He was watching, as if from another room, as the devil beat his form. Then the evilness looked up and saw him. The devil lunged and was hovering over him in an instant.

"Please, don't," he cried.

Daniel cowered, turning his back and bracing for the strike. The rage the devil expelled turned the room a bright red. It glowed in the darkness and shadows played on the walls, like flames flickering in a fire but there was no heat.

It was cold actually and Daniel began to shiver. He rubbed his arms with his hands to get warm but it didn't work. Daniel felt his legs going numb and he was getting weak. His body slumped to the ground and he couldn't move. He heard the devil laugh and say, "Now, you won't get away from me, boy."

Daniel could see the frost from the devil's breath as he laughed into the cold air. The colors changed and were blue and silver and ice crystals accumulated everywhere he looked. He was freezing and had no strength. The devil was taking it from him and he was at the monster's mercy. God help him, but he thought he was dying. The devil had sucked the life from him and all he could do was watch and wait for the end.

"Help me, please," Daniel moaned.

The devil's laugh began to echo and Daniel's vision was blurring. He was sweating suddenly. How could that be? He was so cold that he couldn't feel anything. The air was getting thick and he was having trouble breathing. Then the devil brought up his fist and waved it under Daniel's nose. Smoke billowed from the clenched fingers, filling Daniel's nostrils and choking him.

Gasping and coughing, his eyes watered and his vision became worse. "If you can't breathe now, just wait," the devil's voice rasped, and he raised his fist higher to strike and everything went black.

"No!" Daniel screamed, sitting up in bed.

He was clenching the sheets in fisted hands and Bob was sitting next to him, ears up and staring. The dog whimpered, pawing at Daniel, as if trying to wake him. As Daniel's eyes focused, he realized he'd just had another nightmare. He put his arms around the dog and pulled him close, rubbing behind the animal's ears. "Sorry I woke you up, Bob. That was a bad one."

The dog told Daniel it was okay by licking his hands and getting as close as his body could, the tip of his tail wagging slightly. Bob had been there through all of the nightmares and Daniel thought he had some sort of sixth sense about them. He knew how they affected Daniel and his worried little face always greeted Daniel out of the dream, brows furrowed and eyes searching intently. When Bob was certain Daniel was awake, he always felt the need to comfort.

"You're a good dog, Bob. I don't know what I'd do without you," Daniel said, kissing the top of the dog's head. Bob sighed in contentment, happy to be wrapped in Daniel's arms and knowing his world was okay again.

A light knock came from Daniel's bedroom door and it opened slowly. Frank peeked his head around the door. "A rough night?" he asked.

"Yeah, pretty bad. I haven't had one in a while," he replied.

"Need some air?" Frank asked.

"Yes," Daniel nodded.

They drove the truck through the night with Frank behind the wheel and Bob sitting in the middle. Daniel let the breeze from the open passenger window hit him in the face, calming his nerves and soothing his stomach. He was already feeling better.

"Where're we going?" Frank asked.

"We can go to the place I always go. By the old kiva. We might see Espíritu's band up there," Daniel answered.

They drove to the abandoned kiva and parked. Daniel made Bob stay in the truck in case they encountered any of Espíritu's herd. Since the horses were people-shy, they probably wouldn't react well to a dog, particularly if Bob decided to bark about something.

Daniel held the flashlight and Frank rested a shotgun on his shoulder, a reminder that Daniel hadn't done that in the past but should in the future. Frank also left the truck's headlights on to give them better light. They unlocked the sanctuary gate.

"You can never be too careful," Frank said.

"I know. I'm ready to try shooting again. If you are," Daniel added.

"Let me dig out the body armor first," Frank drawled, raising his eyes.

"It was pretty pathetic, wasn't it?" Daniel grinned.

"Well, I would say I've seen worse, but I really haven't," Frank teased.

Daniel laughed. "It sure showed you could move pretty fast for an old man," he shot back.

"Yeah, I've still got it. For an old man," Frank replied, smiling.

"Listen," Daniel said suddenly, raising the flashlight.

As if on cue, Daniel's light found the magnificent stallion. The horse was standing about thirty feet from them, its ears up and staring in their direction. He showed no intention of moving, indicating he was being as cautious as he was curious. The rest of his herd lingered behind him, a few grazing and the remainder watching their leader's response to the intruders.

"Espíritu," Daniel coaxed, "remember me?"

The horse's ears swiveled in Daniel's direction and he snorted, but stood his ground. He wasn't ready to come closer. Espíritu's head jerked higher. He eyed Frank and Daniel, as if in a standoff, daring either one of them to move. Daniel thought something appeared different in the horse's manner. He was on alert as if sensing danger and Daniel knew it wasn't from them. Something else was bothering the stallion.

"Something's not right," whispered Daniel.

"He does seem a little prickly," Frank said.

The mood of the horse caused Frank to glance around them. Something about it made the hair on the back of his neck stand up. He hoped a predator wasn't stalking nearby but to be safe they needed to slowly get back to the truck. Any sudden or quick movements could cause whatever was lurking to attack. It was risky ignoring the horses, but their safety was first. Once inside the truck, they might be able to help the herd.

Before Frank could say anything to Daniel, the entire band became aware of danger. Everything happened quickly. Espíritu reared up on his hind legs and let out a high-pitched neigh. That caused Daniel to turn and then Frank saw it. A mountain lion was crouched in the shadows ready to spring. It was the biggest cougar Frank had ever seen and the cat was positioned between Daniel and the stallion.

Frank had no time to think. He could only react. The animal let out a low growl and sprang forward. Frank stepped up, yelling at Daniel to stay put. The blast from the shotgun shattered the silence of the night and the herd of horses scattered. The big cat lay dead on the ground.

Neither Frank nor Daniel moved for the longest time. The reality of what could have happened lingered just long enough for them to realize how lucky they were. Eventually Frank found his voice.

"Are you okay, Daniel?" he asked.

"Yes. Are you?"

Frank nodded and walked over to the animal. He figured it measured about six feet in length. What a shame, Frank thought. Such a beautiful creature but he had no choice. And if they hadn't been there, some of the horses could have been killed. He'd report it in the morning.

"Do you think there are others?" Daniel asked.

"Probably not. Mountain lions are usually solitary animals," Frank replied.

"You're a good shot," Daniel said.

"It's a good thing," Frank replied.

They went back to the truck and found Bob waiting patiently for them. His wagging tail told them how happy he was they had returned. Frank wondered if this same cat had been the cause of Ed Tate's problems. Surely someone would've come across the remains of the missing horse if it had been attacked. He hadn't heard one way or another. As for the bite marks on Tate's other horse, anyone could tell you they could've easily come from one of Ed's own horses. Ed Tate was stretching with that one.

Espíritu's band hadn't grown. He still had the same number in his harem as he always had, so Espíritu couldn't have lured Tate's mare away. There was still no sign of the man's horse mingling with any of the sanctuary herds. Frank was diligent in checking.

Frank glanced at Daniel sitting in the truck. Terror had gripped his heart when he saw the cougar, and when the cat lunged, he wasn't certain if it was going for Daniel or the stallion. All Frank knew was that he had to stop it and he had a split second to do it. He doesn't want to think about what might have happened if he'd missed. His son was safe. It felt good to say it. His son.

———

James Tate was agitated. How could he have been so stupid? He had promised himself that the gambling would end. When the last debt had been paid off, he pledged no more gambling. He couldn't afford it. Selling his dad's mare was risky and now he found himself in another hole. One little bet led to another. And another. Now he was up to his ears and owed much more than the last time. He was cursed and he didn't know what to do about it.

Beating up that little punk Joe helped. He'd taken great pleasure in taking out his frustrations on the Indian kid. Funny, the kid didn't even put up a fight. It was as if he just wanted to get it over with. Well, James was happy to oblige. He smirked at the thought. He had threatened Joe within in an inch of his life, his family's life and Maria's life that if he squealed, he would hurt them, too. So there was no threat of retaliation from the great Daniel.

There was a problem though. One of the counselors at the school recognized James. It happened right after he had finished his business with Joe. James nearly ran into the man as he was making a getaway. The counselor looked right at him and asked what he was doing at the school. Fortunately, another teacher had found Joe crumpled behind the building at that time and called out to the man for help. James used that as a means of escape. He wasn't sure if the counselor would put him at the scene of the crime, but it was a possibility.

He was going to need an alibi and wasn't sure who that might be. If he could find someone to lie for him, then it could be James' word against the counselor's if he happened to get questioned. The only other possibility would be snitching on the one person who could verify why he was at the school in the first place. That wouldn't help him any since he'd be implementing himself in illegal activity. Any way James looked at it, he was in a predicament. He was up to his neck in a few things and probably the only person who could possibly help him would be his dad. But that would require confessing about the mare for starters. James wasn't ready to do that just yet.

Whatever he came up with, he'd need to do it quickly. James was starting to get a little paranoid about his own safety. He'd already been threatened with bodily harm if he didn't pay up soon, so it was only a matter of time before the thugs he chose to do business with came calling.

Some positive news had been shared with him. James casually mentioned to his dad that it was strange no one knew where Daniel had come from. That's all it took. Old man Tate ran off with that little tidbit like a dog with a bone about to hide it in the garden. He knew whatever Daniel ran from or was hiding would soon surface due to Ed Tate's hatred for Frank Carpenter. His dad's private investigators would see to it. James smiled at the thought of seeing Daniel's face when his past caught up with him. And he had every intention of being there when it happened.

CHAPTER ELEVEN

Sarah's meeting went well. Her idea to use their horses for the therapy program had been kindly received by the physical therapists at the hospital. It was going better than she had planned. The possibility of having something started by this time next year was likely.

There was something on her mind she had failed to mention to Frank. She meant to discuss it with him last night but he'd been tired from working in the hay fields. The first cutting had been successful and there was a lot to discuss from all of that work. What she had to say could wait but she felt it was something to think about, not something to worry about necessarily, but something they should discuss as parents.

Parents. That word that had been so elusive in their lives was now staring them in the face. The issue involved Daniel and what she'd seen on her way home from the market a few days ago.

It had been twilight when she reached the outskirts of their property. Often she took the longer route home because it allowed her to pass their old house. Seeing it always made her remember the lean years and allowed her to appreciate just how far they had come. The house stood empty but there were times over the years that she and Frank rented it out for various reasons. When they had extended ranch help, the house also provided a temporary home to the workers.

No one was currently living in it, so the lights she saw from a front window caught her attention. She slowed her SUV, thinking there might be intruders. The house was some distance from the road and cottonwood trees lined the property, shielding her car. Whoever was in their house wouldn't be able to see her easily. She waited for about ten minutes but it seemed an eternity.

Then just as she was about to give up and rush home to call the police, Daniel emerged from the house holding Maria's hand. She watched the familiar and casual way they touched and saw them walk around to the back of the house. Sarah realized they had probably parked behind the house and she decided to drive away as quickly as possible. She didn't want to encounter them on the road.

As she drove the rest of the way, she wondered what their responsibilities as parents were. Sarah wasn't naïve. She knew Daniel and Maria had been intimate simply by the way they touched each other. The empty house provided a place for them to be alone.

She wasn't angry, just baffled as to how to handle a situation they'd never been in before. She'd never had the privilege of diapering her own baby and here she was wondering if her soon to be son was using birth control. Normal parents had the luxury of enjoying their child through the years, relishing the good and addressing the challenging in stages. It wasn't something Sarah felt comfortable ignoring. She almost laughed anticipating the look on Frank's face when she told him.

Later that night, Sarah had her opportunity. She was soaking in a bubble bath with candles lit and soft music playing. It was a relaxing luxury that she didn't allow herself to enjoy enough. Her husband walked in carrying a glass of wine for her.

"Thought you might like this," Frank said, handing her the glass.

"Thank you," she began, "Frank, I need to talk to you about something."

"I'm all ears," he replied.

"Well, it's probably not anything, but do you ever think about the birds and the bees?" she blurted.

Frank's amused eyes didn't miss a beat. "Every day, darlin'. And if that's a proposition, it's the strangest one from you yet."

Sarah laughed out loud. "No, that's not what I mean," she said, smiling at her husband. "That didn't come out right."

"Well, damn. A man can only hope. If you change your mind, I can be in that tub in nothin' flat," he replied, his eyes twinkling.

Sarah then told him what she'd seen the other day at their old house. She shared her thoughts about Daniel and Maria and wondered aloud what they should do. Frank sat on her vanity stool, listening intently, his face registering everything she was saying by raised eyebrows and widened eyes. She loved her husband's expressive face.

He didn't respond immediately. Sarah finally said, "Frank, say something."

"We didn't even go through potty training," Frank mused, looking up.

"Or teething," Sarah said.

"Or the first day of school," he grinned, moving to the side of the tub.

"Or his first school concert," she giggled, as he kissed her neck.

"I did teach him how to drive though," Frank said into her ear.

"And to ride a horse," she replied.

"I suppose that means we should talk to him about the birds and the bees then," he said, looking up at his wife.

"You," Sarah began, "you should talk to him."

"Me?" he asked.

"Yes, you. He's almost nineteen. Don't you think it'll be a little embarrassing for him if I did it?" she asked.

"It'll be a little embarrassing for me if I do it. Besides, I'm sure he knows all about the deed anyway," Frank said, smiling.

"You know what I mean. About protection," she said.

"I know what you mean," he said, sighing.

"We wanted to be parents," Sarah said, touching the side of his face.

"Yeah, I know. You sure you don't want to be the one to talk to him?" he asked.

"Certain," she reassured him.

"Isn't that water getting a little cold?" Frank asked, changing the subject, his eyes growing dark.

"Pretty much. I'm turning into a prune," she replied.

"Can't let that happen," he murmured. Frank grabbed a towel and held it up for her as she stood, wrapping the softness around her wet skin. He held her like that until the tub drained. Then he blew out the candles and they walked to their bedroom.

———

Maria was supposed to be helping Merrill with inventory but her mind kept wandering. Thoughts of Daniel filled her head and distracted her. She kept thinking of the time they had spent together in the Carpenters' old house. At first she'd been a little nervous. She couldn't help feeling as if they were trespassing or doing something dishonest. It was clear Daniel felt that way, too, but after a while, they both were able to relax.

He had brought her flowers. It was the first bouquet she'd ever been given. Daniel took one flower from the bunch, broke the stem and slid the bloom behind her ear. Then he kissed her and all thoughts about being discovered in the empty house rushed from her head. All she could think of was the way his lips touched her own, how her skin tingled at his touch and the way she lost all sense of being. Then her thought process disappeared and she allowed her sense of touch to guide her. It was beautiful and something she could never have imagined.

"Maria," her father called, interrupting her thoughts.

"Yes, Papa?" she responded.

"Don't forget that box over there," he reminded, pointing to a bin containing cans of sauce.

"I won't," she replied.

"Are you okay?" Merrill asked, hands on hips and staring at his daughter.

"I'm fine. I didn't sleep very well," she lied. Her father's worried face looked very tired, she thought, and she felt guilty.

Merrill started to turn away but changed his mind and turned to his daughter. "Just how serious is it with Daniel?"

"I like him, Papa," she replied simply, surprised at the question. No other answer came to her.

"I see," Merrill said, nodding. He turned again to walk away but Maria stopped him.

"I'm still going to college, Papa. That hasn't changed."

"Good," he said, looking a little relieved and he left the room.

Maria knew her father was a man of few words but his body language often made him easy to read. She realized it had taken a lot for him to ask her about Daniel and she was aware he'd been worried about her. He liked Daniel, that she was certain.

Merrill had missed out on much of Maria's life. It hadn't been easy for the man to lose his wife and child to divorce and still live with the customs he believed in. He never remarried, instead devoting the rest of his life to running his restaurant and bar. He listened to the hard luck stories of his fellow Navajo when the only thing that would dull reality for them would be a visit to Merrill's bar. Merrill related because he lived it, too.

———

Daniel thought Frank was acting strangely. He'd barely said "good morning" to Daniel and did so by looking down at his boots. Frank always greeted him heartily and directly, looking him straight in the eye. He'd had his moods before but nothing like this. The man had gone out of his way to avoid Daniel all morning.

He was beginning to get a little worried and wondered if he should ask if something was wrong when Frank came around the corner of the barn. He stopped in front of Daniel and stared blankly, as if he wanted to say something but didn't know how. He then cleared his throat and walked away again. This happened three more times until Daniel decided to go to the opposite end of the barn to see what happened. Sure enough, Frank went back to the spot where Daniel had been standing, realized he wasn't there and walked away.

"Well, that's it," Daniel murmured, determined to seek out Frank and ask what was going on.

He found him pitching hay onto the back of a trailer, moving with the speed of someone in a race with time. Sweat glistened on Frank's face and he stopped working long enough to remove his hat and wipe his brow on the back of his sleeve.

"Is there a rush or something?" Daniel asked, startling Frank.

"Just want to get it done," Frank replied, glancing at Daniel.

"Is there something you want to say to me?" Daniel asked.

"Why do you ask?" Frank responded.

"It's kind of obvious," Daniel stated.

"Why's that?" Frank asked.

"Well, you've been marching around the barn for the last hour and you don't normally march," Daniel said.

"Doesn't mean I have anything to say," Frank mumbled, hands on hips.

"Good grief," Daniel replied.

"It's kind of awkward," Frank said suddenly as if he needed to get Daniel's attention.

"What is?" asked Daniel.

"What I have to say," he replied.

"Just spill it," said Daniel. It seemed that morning the roles had been reversed, where Daniel was the adult with Frank being afraid to confess something to him.

Taking a deep breath, Frank said, "Let's walk."

The two of them walked side by side, not saying a word. Daniel had no idea where they were going but stayed in step with Frank. The man seemed to visibly relax as he went, either clearing his head or gaining courage, Daniel wasn't sure which but it was obvious Frank wasn't as worked up.

They reached a clearing that was scented with sagebrush, the plant concealing the earth like a silvery carpet. In the distance, a band of horses grazed and lounged, unaware they were being watched by the two of them.

"You like Maria," Frank said, not asking. He stared out over the sanctuary land at the horses.

"Yes," Daniel replied.

"That's good," came Frank's reply. He still didn't look at Daniel.

"Yes, it is," confirmed Daniel.

"You know about protection, right?" Frank asked, glancing his way.

It took a minute for Daniel to realize where Frank was going with what he had to say. No wonder he'd been tongue-tied.

"I do," he said.

"That's good. It's important," Frank nodded, watching the horses.

"Yes, I know," said Daniel.

"And," Frank hesitated, "important to use consistently."

"Okay," Daniel said, nodding.

After briefly hesitating, Frank turned to Daniel, pushing his hat back from his brow and scratching his head. Daniel had seen him do that in the past when he had trouble finding the right words for something he thought was important.

"Daniel, this parenting thing is obviously new to me and Sarah, so we'll probably hit a few snags along the way. Mess up real good sometimes, too," Frank said.

"You haven't so far," Daniel replied, the memory of what he'd known too close to the surface.

"Well, we also realize you're an adult, so there's just so much wisdom we can shoot your way," he smiled. "But as an adult, you have an obligation to be responsible and accountable. To yourself and to Maria."

"I understand that," said Daniel.

"Good. I knew you understood. Just felt I needed to say it all. As a parent," Frank said, looking back at the horses.

"I'm glad you did," Daniel said. He watched the man who had provided a new beginning for him. The man who acknowledged him as a son, and the father who found it embarrassing to discuss an awkward topic with his son, but knew he had to.

"Was I really marching?" Frank asked suddenly, turning to Daniel.

"Yeah, you really were," replied Daniel, smiling.

"Nah," Frank mumbled.

"High-stepping some," Daniel said, nodding.

"High-stepping?" he asked, eyebrows raised.

"Pretty much. I was beginning to wonder if you'd been in a marching band in high school," Daniel said.

"I can't even play a damn instrument," Frank said.

"But you know how to march," Daniel replied, laughing. "Pretty well, I might add."

"Better to not share any of that with Sarah, 'cause I'll just deny it," Frank said.

They then watched as another band of horses galloped into the setting, stopping just in time to view the first band at a distance. The first herd decided it was time to move on, following its stallion and trotting out of sight. The second herd decided to graze a little, while a couple of the horses rolled around on their backs, a dust cloud forming around them.

As Daniel looked at the horses, he was reminded of the incident with the mountain lion, and how close to harm he'd been. How tragic things could have turned out for these beautiful animals if it hadn't been for Frank's quick actions. But Frank saved the horses from possible slaughter in the first place by offering a safe haven for them to live. He was a man who wouldn't take any credit for doing something good. Frank would just say it was the right thing to do.

A father, not by blood, but by heart.

CHAPTER TWELVE

Joe had healed enough to start visiting Daniel at the ranch again. The bruises had faded and the swelling was gone. Since it was summer, he often came over in the mornings with Bill, and watched as the work got done around the ranch, the alfalfa fields and the sanctuary. He'd pitch in when he could, staying until the afternoons when Inez would drop him off at the Turnout, where he worked most evenings.

Bill and Inez hovered over Joe, worried that their son was too delicate to function and that he might overexert himself with the slightest effort. Joe wore the fragility tag his parents placed on him with patience but Daniel saw moments where his friend was on the verge of yelling at the ones who loved him most.

Daniel still tried to coerce his friend into confessing who had beaten him up. Joe never budged.

"I don't see why you won't report it," Daniel said, one day in the barn.

"Don't want to, Daniel," Joe replied.

"Well, I know James Tate was behind it," said Daniel.

"No, you don't," Joe said.

"It doesn't make any sense, keeping it quiet," Daniel mumbled.

"It makes perfect sense. To me," Joe said. "Besides, it's too late now."

"It's never too late," Daniel retorted.

"Can we just change the subject or something?" Joe asked.

"Okay. Tell me what it's like to have a medicine man come to your house," Daniel said, grinning.

"Lots of chanting and stones and stuff," Joe replied.

"Stones?" he asked.

"Well, none were thrown, if that's what you're thinking," Joe smiled.

"So you were chanting and stuff for two weeks?" Daniel asked.

"I wasn't chanting, but yes, pretty much," Joe said.

"Seems kind of long," Daniel said.

"Those healing ceremonies can get a little long," Joe smirked.

"But, it's part of your culture, as Maria would say," Daniel reminded him.

"Yes, it is. The culture that drives me crazy and even crazier when my parents won't back off," Joe said.

"They're just worried about you, Joe. We all are," Daniel said to his friend.

"I know, I know," he said, a little annoyed.

"So what do you want to talk about?" Daniel asked, changing the subject. He knew pushing Joe was making him irritable.

"I hear you're shooting again. How's that going?" Joe asked, his eyes lighting up.

"Actually, much better than the first time," Daniel laughed.

"You know it wouldn't take much to improve that one," he said.

"I've hit a target or two," smiled Daniel.

"Not a person, right? You haven't shot anyone I hope," Joe quipped.

"No, not a person, thank you very much," Daniel said.

"I think I'm ready to try riding again, Daniel," Joe said abruptly.

"Okay. Any reason?" asked Daniel, surprised.

"It's time, I think. I've got to quit being such a coward," Joe said.

"Would you stop it? You aren't a coward," Daniel exclaimed.

"I am really. I'm afraid of horses. I get myself beat up. I'm scared of life," Joe said.

"You had a reason to fear horses and you didn't get yourself anything. That blame goes to James Tate," said Daniel.

"Ladies and gentlemen, meet Joe, the coward," Joe said, raising his voice and taking a bow to an imaginary audience.

"I can saddle up a horse for you anytime you're ready," Daniel said, wishing he could get through to his friend.

"Do me a favor. Give me one of those old, gentle ones, will you? And I need to learn to saddle my own horse, by the way," Joe said.

"Yes, you do, and I'll teach you," Daniel said gently.

Daniel didn't know what was going on with Joe, but he'd changed. He was happy his friend was willing to give horseback riding another chance, but knew it would be a long process for him to lose the fear, if he ever did.

"Oh, by the way, don't mention it to the 'rents," Joe said.

"I won't say anything, but there's a good chance Bill will notice. He does work here," Daniel reminded him.

"I'll figure something out," said Joe.

The two of them thought of some possible times for Joe to ride, namely when Bill would be off work. Daniel didn't like going behind anyone's back. He'd felt guilty using Frank and Sarah's house without their knowledge just to be alone with Maria. He suspected they found out about it, which led to Frank's talk with him. It was never mentioned, but Daniel was relieved with the possibility they knew. He didn't feel as if they were sneaking around anymore. It was Joe's call to keep the knowledge he was riding from his parents. Daniel had to respect his wishes.

———

Frank had endured a grueling day in the hay fields. It was hot and he was miserable. It didn't help that he and Daniel also had to repair a section of fencing around the sanctuary. He wasn't sure if it was vandalism, but he wasn't ruling it out. His back ached from all of the work and he couldn't wait to take a relaxing shower.

He was noticing the little aches and pains that came more frequently. It was hard to acknowledge the physical labor of running the ranch wasn't as easy on his body as it used to be. But the pain reminded him. His joints got stiff and his shoulders hurt. Arthritis had touched Frank Carpenter and it pissed him off. He had no intention of giving up for a long time, but he also knew there would come a time when the torch would have to be passed. It eased his mind that Daniel would be there to take it.

As he came from the barn, he noticed a Bureau of Land Management truck pulling up his drive. Walt Wright got out of the vehicle and walked toward Frank.

"Boy, it's a hot one today," Walt said.

"It sure is," Frank replied, shaking the man's hand.

"Got some news you might be interested in," Walt said.

"Come on in the house and let's get something to drink," Frank replied, leading Walt into the kitchen.

"Water, tea, lemonade, soft drinks, what's your pleasure? Sarah keeps us well stocked," he said, looking in the refrigerator. "Or would you rather have a beer?"

"Water's fine," Walt said.

The two men sat at the kitchen table, enjoying the coolness of the house. Frank looked at Walt expectantly.

"It's been brought to my attention that Ed Tate's mare was sold to Bain's Rodeo," Walt confirmed.

"What? Why would Ed do such a thing?" Frank asked.

"Ed didn't. James did," said Walt.

"How did you find out?" asked Frank.

"Let's just say one thing led to another. Apparently, James Tate has a little gambling problem. He needed money to pay off a debt and sold the mare. Of course, he let Ed think your horses were responsible," Walt explained.

"And of course, Ed wouldn't believe otherwise without proof," Frank mused, rubbing his temples. A headache now added to his pain.

"I've heard the horse was bought for Bain's daughter. Maybe to breed, I don't really know. But it's not being used in the rodeo. It just shares a paddock with some of the other mares," Walt added.

"So if we went to one of his weekly rodeo shows, we might see it?" Frank asked.

"Yes. They're kept out behind the stands, in full view. A photo might help," Walt hinted, nodding.

"Well, that won't be easy. Bain doesn't allow cameras at his shows," Frank reminded him.

"You have a cell phone, right? With a camera? Just be discreet," said Walt.

"I'll have to think about this, Walt," Frank replied. His head was spinning.

"This is good news, right? Might not be easy to prove, but proof is what you need to get Tate to back off his accusations," Walt said.

"Why can't we just go to Bain and ask if James sold him the horse?" asked Frank.

"I've heard his daughter is spoiled rotten and had to have the horse the moment she saw it. Bain didn't actually buy it for her. One of the rodeo hands bought it for himself after James approached him with it, but when the daughter laid eyes on the horse, she had to have it," Walt explained.

"And Bain paid off the rodeo hand," Frank added.

"That's about the gist of it," Walt added.

"Let me guess. The rodeo hand wasn't too happy about it and did a little singing?" Frank asked, raising his eyebrows and looking directly at Walt.

"You didn't hear from me," Walt conceded.

"Then why not have the guy who bought the horse from James in the first place confess to Ed?" Frank asked.

"It gets a little complicated. Bain fired this kid, too, by the way. Turns out the kid was so angry, he confided in a friend hoping to find a way to at least get his job back. The friend is a counselor at the high school. Apparently, James Tate was seen often at the school and was suspected of being involved in a gambling ring some detectives had been trying to bust," Walt explained.

"So the former rodeo employee is a witness somehow?" Frank asked.

"Yes. James admitted to him that he had to sell the horse to pay off a debt," Walt said. "And there's something else."

Frank waited for the man to continue.

"That counselor at the school suspects James was responsible for beating up a student on school grounds," Walt added.

"Why?" Frank asked sharply, thinking of Joe.

"Saw him. James was rounding the building, red in the face and out of breath, just as the other kid was discovered. Didn't see it happen, but it looked pretty suspicious to the man," Walt said.

"We know the boy that got beaten up," Frank said. He explained the connection to Walt.

"I'm sorry, Frank. It's too bad that Joe won't reveal James for the bullying thug he is," Walt said.

"Daniel seems to think James threatened his family. I tend to agree," he said.

"Well, that seems logical. Think about the rodeo, Frank. And remember, you didn't hear any of this from me," Walt said, standing up.

"I appreciate you taking the time to come out here," Frank told the man.

"Anytime. Hey, I'm on your side," Walt said.

They walked outside and stood talking when another truck made its way up the drive. Frank didn't recognize the driver until the vehicle was parked beside Walt's BLM truck. The robust figure behind the wheel was unmistakable. Frank's headache intensified. He was having one hell of a day, he thought.

"Well, now, conspiring, are we?" Ed Tate's voice boomed the distance as he got out of his truck.

"What can I do for you, Ed?" Frank asked through clenched teeth.

"You can keep your damn horses on your own property, that's what you can do," Ed fumed.

"My horses are on my property, Ed. All accounted for," Frank said.

"Well, they don't stay there, my friend," Ed retorted.

"Ed, I'm tired of these baseless allegations. My horses are not your problem," Frank hinted, wanting very badly to spill everything Walt had just told him, knowing he couldn't.

"They're my problem if they lure my property away. Another mare is missing, along with a gelding," Ed said.

"Listen to what you're saying, Ed. A mare maybe, but a stallion isn't going to lure a gelding," Frank said patiently.

"But the mare's still missing," huffed Ed, still trying to prove his point.

"Daniel and I killed a mountain lion not too long ago," Frank said, offering another possibility to the man.

"I heard," Ed said.

"Well, have you noticed any blood anywhere? Have you searched all your property?" Frank asked.

"None and yes," the man fumed.

"Have you noticed any scavengers? If the horses ran and were attacked, well the carcass would attract them," Walt offered.

"You think I don't know that?" yelled Ed.

"Ed, you need to leave. This is getting out of control," Frank said.

"Oh, I'm just getting started," the man laughed.

"That's not the first time you've threatened me. Here's something for you to chew on. Keep your son away from my horses and off my land. He's done enough damage," Frank said, nearly spitting every word at the man.

"Your land. Your horses. That's rich, coming from someone who doesn't belong here," Ed mimicked. "I ought to take my gun and kill every single wild horse you have. They don't belong here any more than you do, or that fake son of yours."

"Ed, leave now. You've crossed the line. I'll call the sheriff if I have to," Walt yelled.

"Who the hell are you ordering me around? I should've got you fired when I had the chance," Ed screamed. "The sheriff? I might just have a tidbit or two to share with him about old Daniel."

Frank and Walt watched as he got in his truck and sped off, throwing gravel with his tires while a dust trail followed behind. Frank had no idea what the man had meant in reference to Daniel. It was yet another threat Ed Tate was fond of spewing at him. But Daniel had done nothing to warrant the sheriff getting involved, unless he was being framed for something. He'd ask Daniel about it and warn him to be on the lookout for any trouble. The last thing Frank wanted was to see his son accused of something he hadn't done.

CHAPTER THIRTEEN

Sarah loved when she could drive the sanctuary land on her own. Often she'd find a herd grazing and she would get out of the SUV and just watch. The grace and beauty of the magnificent animals left her speechless. She understood why saving these wild horses meant so much to Frank. Pride emanated from these creatures with their every movement, as if they understood the role they played in history and what they represented.

She grabbed her camera and started shooting photos of a couple of yearlings frolicking in the grass. The two youngsters ran around each other, often rearing on their hind legs in playful combat, one a beautiful bay color with a black mane and tail, the other a red roan, its flaxen tail and matching mane shining in the sunlight.

The two nipped and danced, strutting around each other, tails and heads held high. They ran to and fro, turning sharply and leisurely, practicing for a time when those skills would be needed. But for the moment, they enjoyed the carefree joy found in youth.

Suddenly the two were alerted that the rest of the band was ready to move. The herd advanced as one, a palette of equine color blurred the landscape, grulla, buckskin, bay, chestnut and dun mixed with sorrel, roan, black, brown and white. A masterpiece for the moment, an image made only by nature to be seen by a fortunate few. Sarah readily admitted none of her digital images would replicate the splendor.

As she put her camera away, she thought of what Frank told her about the Tates. Walt's information had provided some peace of mind, but that knowledge wouldn't stop Ed's threats. It didn't seem right that they had to prove anything to the brute since they hadn't done anything wrong. Particularly since it involved attending a rodeo, something Sarah detested. But she would go with Frank and Daniel, if only to look out for them as they got whatever information they needed to substantiate James Tate's guilt.

———

Interesting news reached the devil. At first, he thought his deteriorating hearing had deceived him. A man cornered him one day in the parking lot of his favorite bar. Immediately suspicious, the devil turned ready to fight. But the fight left his failing body long ago. And that made him angrier. He wanted to punch the guy's nose until it bled, just for the hell of it. But he barely had the strength to lift a glass to his mouth, much less move any muscle with force.

A doctor at the clinic told him he had liver cancer. The devil didn't believe it or maybe he just didn't care. He continued to drink the remainder of his life away, erasing reality with intoxication. Delusions intensified.

But the stranger told him a story. Surely it was true and he hadn't imagined it. Something about that good for nothing son of his being located. In all honesty, the devil had forgotten about the little bastard. Good riddance. Oh, he was mad as hell at first. He remembered that. He probably would have killed the kid if he'd gotten his hands on him. As time went on, however, the devil grew to like the independence. No brat around needing something from him. He came and went as he pleased and that was fine with him.

So he wasn't sure what he thought about the latest revelation. He wasn't even sure what he wanted to do about it. Common sense told him to let it go. But he'd never had much common sense. He couldn't quite remember, but the boy would probably be an adult by now, so the devil could do very little. But his pride got the better of him and made his anger fester. The little punk had tricked him and that made him want to hurt the boy more than ever.

His mind wandered to his late wife. Sometimes he imagined she was still there with him. They'd been happy once. At least he had, what he knew of happiness anyway. It wasn't until the brat came and he'd discovered his wife's true feelings for that man. Charley, wasn't it? Then he lost all control and the rage overtook him most times. He couldn't help it. He didn't like the meanness but that was deep inside him. He'd thought of putting a bullet in his head a number of times just to ease the turmoil, but he didn't have the courage. So he took it out on everyone else around him. It was that hatred that wouldn't go away.

His vision clouded a bit. He saw the man, Charley. He was laughing with the devil's wife, touching her face. He wanted to scream at them to stop, but he watched through the haze, no sound coming from his mouth. And they held a baby in their arms. Was that the brat? The devil couldn't remember. Why was that? He wanted to punch the wall, yell, do anything to remember, but he couldn't. His head pounded.

She hadn't loved him and made that clear every chance she got. He did remember that. And he wanted to hurt her like she hurt him. He'd used his fist some and the back of his hand. She'd spit and kick and punch.

The violence seemed never ending and was eventually directed toward the boy. He couldn't stand the noise the kid made. The crying was incessant and nearly drove him mad. The devil reached up to cover his ears as if that would make the memory of it go away. She wouldn't make it stop. So it was up to him although he only seemed to make it worse when the boy was young.

But the kid got tough and took it. Like a man. Just like the devil had. Until that day when they put his wife in the ground and the kid stood up to him. If the devil hadn't passed out, there was no telling what would've happened.

He thought the boy stood taller than him at the time, but he wasn't sure. Maybe his memory was playing tricks, as with everything else. But didn't he think once or twice that the kid could probably hurt him if he'd wanted to? Why hadn't he? Maybe he would have that last time.

The devil was tired. He should sleep on all the new information and maybe he could make a better decision later, when his mind wasn't so cloudy. The problem was he couldn't remember when his mind had been clear.

He closed his eyes. If he were lucky, he wouldn't wake up. But he'd never been the lucky sort, and didn't suspect much to change for him now.

CHAPTER FOURTEEN

Frank parked Sarah's SUV in the lot. He looked at his wife sitting next to him and knew this was the last place on earth she wanted to be. Living out west all of these years never lessened her dislike for rodeos, even though they were widely accepted and enjoyed events by most everyone they knew. She was here for him, plain and simple. He reached over and squeezed her hand. She looked at him and smiled.

He glanced in his rear view mirror at Daniel and Maria sitting in the back seat. They wore worried expressions on their faces. Frank knew they weren't too thrilled to be here either, particularly under these circumstances.

"You all ready?" he asked.

Daniel met his eyes in the mirror and nodded.

"Okay, then. Let's go," Frank said, getting out of the vehicle.

They walked up to the gate and handed their tickets in at the admission counter. Frank had remembered to purchase tickets in advance as the shows often sold out. Tourists pretty much kept it in operation on a weekly basis, otherwise it couldn't sustain itself and the shows would be fewer.

Bain had hit on a tourist jackpot, Frank admitted. People from all over the world thought Bain's shows represented the American southwest and how the populace lived today. Nothing could be further from the truth. It was sort of like Times Square in New York, simply a tourist destination for something to do but wasn't anything like the area or the rest of the country. Both were cheesy, gimmicky, tacky and a big misrepresentation of what life was for most people, in his opinion.

Yes, rodeos have been around a long time and for the most part do exhibit skills that ranchers employ from their workers. Minus the flash and sometimes questionable treatment of the animals, Frank really didn't have a problem with them. However he knew how some of the horses were obtained dirt cheap from the rez auctions and that hadn't made him happy. At least they weren't kill buyers.

But the animal issue was the sole reason Bain prevented cameras. There were people who boycotted rodeos all over the country because they believed the owners engaged in unethical treatment of the animals. Bain wasn't about to be shut down by protesters.

This was mainly Sarah's problem with them, although she didn't care for the young children participating in some of the events either. She argued a child had no business around a bull or barrel racing without a helmet. It was too dangerous. He had to agree with her.

It was a full house, Frank observed. They squeezed through a crowd of people who spoke languages Frank didn't understand. Some wore brand new cowboy hats just purchased from a souvenir stand, while carrying little American flags. Gathering from the tour buses pulling in the parking lot, more were on the way. If this was supposed to represent the American west, there weren't many locals in attendance. Frank nearly laughed out loud at the irony.

Signs indicated seating was full on the near side, so they moved with the flow toward the other side of the outdoor arena. This was good because, if Frank remembered correctly, the paddocks were located in the back. They reached the ramp that would lead them to their seats, and just behind it were untacked horses, secured in locked pens.

"See the mare anywhere?" Sarah whispered. She had put her arm through Frank's to get closer so no one would hear.

"I'm not sure," he said, scanning the view of about three dozen horses.

Sarah held her cell phone in her hand and Frank assumed she was taking photos. He glanced at Daniel and Maria and smiled. Daniel had his right arm draped over Maria's shoulders and was casually holding his cell phone in that hand, snapping away while it appeared he was talking to his girlfriend. Frank guessed Maria was doing the same since she was holding a phone, too.

Frank had been the only holdout in the photography quest. If anyone would draw attention to what they were doing, it would be him. He hated to use any phone, much less a mobile one because the things were so small. He had fumble fingers using the devices and was forever dropping them. If they didn't break, they landed in things that destroyed them. Once he accidentally flipped his phone into a pile of horse manure and thought Daniel was going to collapse in hysterics. There was also the time Mac stepped on one after it fell from his pocket. Yes, he'd owned plenty of cell phones over the years, and didn't like any of them. Sarah replaced every one of them for emergency purposes, making him promise to carry it. It had been a unanimous decision, however, to forbid him from even touching one that night.

"Better get to our seats," Sarah said quietly, glancing up the ramp at a security guard who appeared to be watching them.

They moved again, easing into the crowd and traveled up the ramp. The security guard was distracted by some kids who were throwing water balloons off the side of the ramp onto the unsuspecting crowd. He didn't see them pass.

"That was close," Sarah mumbled.

"Remind me to thank those kids for perfect timing," Frank said, smiling.

"You better thank the ones who got soaked, too," Sarah laughed.

He squeezed his wife's hand and led them into the seating area. Finding four empty seats together that didn't have an obstructed view wasn't easy. Frank suspected they wouldn't stay for the entire show anyway, so he wasn't sure if where they sat mattered much. Daniel eyed four together right in the middle of the group of people they walked in with and they sat down. At least they might enjoy the show a little more if surrounded by people they couldn't understand, Frank thought.

"I think I saw it," Daniel whispered, leaning in over Maria, toward Sarah and Frank.

"Are you sure?" Frank asked.

"I think so, in the paddock closest to the ramp," he replied.

"Hopefully we got it," Sarah said, referring to the photos they'd taken.

"Me, too, since it'll be dark soon and anything else will require a flash," Daniel said.

Then the music started and the crowd stood. Pre-recorded versions of "God Bless America" and the "Star Spangled Banner" blared, with most men removing their cowboy hats in respect. Frank noted with amusement that the foreign tourists didn't and probably had no idea it was expected. They waved their little flags instead, obviously happy to be at an American rodeo and trying to blend in, with little success.

The beat of "Coming to America" was next, with two females on horseback entering the ring and carrying American flags. The crowd went wild. When the announcer yelled, "Don't you just love this country," the tourists jumped with enthusiasm, high-fiving each other and waving their flags even more vigorously.

Obviously they could understand, Frank thought. He couldn't help thinking how strange the whole situation was. Glancing to his left, Daniel was leaning in to say something again.

"I'll be right back. Bathroom," he pointed over his shoulder, getting up.

Frank watched Daniel leave. He also noticed the same security guard had eyed them. The man decided to follow Daniel.

The bathrooms were nothing more than port-a-potties located at the bottom of the ramp. Frank decided to follow Daniel and keep an eye out, particularly now that they were being watched for some reason. If Daniel didn't notice the man following, Frank worried he'd try to take some more photos before it got completely dark.

"I'm following Daniel. Stay here with Maria," Frank said to Sarah.

The two women on horseback finally ended their ride, to thunderous applause. The rodeo clown made his way to the center of the arena, with wireless microphone, to begin his part of the show some called "comic relief". The man wore tattered clothes, cowboy boots, a wig with hat, and his face was painted in typical clown fashion.

Frank glanced at Sarah as he was leaving. His wife looked miserable. She referred to the "corny clown" as the absolute worst part of sitting through a rodeo. Her face reflected those feelings, as she rubbed her temples. Frank would have to hurry. He didn't think Sarah would last through the show.

He made his way down the ramp but didn't see Daniel or the security guard. Frank's nerves were on edge. He hesitated at the bottom, unsure if he should wait there or go on a search. Leaning against the rail, he looked out at the horses. Sure enough, Ed Tate's mare was enjoying some hay in the paddock closest to him. At least it looked like the Tate mare in the twilight.

Frank couldn't stand still any longer. He needed to look for Daniel. He wandered under the stands and could hear the sounds of the bulls knocking against the stalls in anger. Must be time for the bull riding. Frank thought the men who attempted those stunts a little crazy. It was dangerous and one misstep could lead to severe injury or death.

Not finding Daniel, he wandered around to the concession stands. Popcorn, cotton candy and roasted almonds scented the air, enticing people with the smells to spend more money, whether they were hungry or not. Seeing no sign of Daniel, he decided to buy Sarah some almonds to make up for leaving her in the stands. He knew it wasn't much but it was a start. She loved roasted almonds.

He made his way back to their seats and Daniel was already there, relaxed as if he'd never left. Daniel nodded at Frank, giving him a thumbs up, indicating whatever he left for had been a success.

They sat through the bronc riders and the barrel racers, more clown humor and some games for the kids. Then Sarah made a proclamation.

"Either buy me more roasted almonds, or take me home," she said, waving the empty bag under his nose.

"Well, if you really want some more almonds," he said, starting to get up.

"Home," she said, pulling his arm.

"Okay, let's go," he said, taking her hand.

The four of them walked from their seats and down the ramp. Other families were leaving, too, and they blended with the people exiting with them. Frank figured they were beating the rest of the crowd by about ten minutes as the show was winding down. They walked through the maze of roped off admission rows, heading toward the front gate when a voice yelled for them to stop.

"Not sure if he's talking to us," Frank said, guiding Sarah and not stopping.

"Yeah, better keep walking," Daniel mumbled, holding Maria's hand tightly.

"Hey!" the voice came with a little more force.

More people started exiting the arena, in a hurry to get to the parking lot and beat the traffic backup that was certain to happen. The voice yelled to the crowd and no one paid attention.

They nearly made it to their SUV when a hand grabbed Daniel's arm, turning him around. The four of them stopped and looked at the security guard. It was the same man who had been watching them all evening. He looked directly at Daniel.

"I kept yelling for you to stop," the man said.

"We're sorry. We didn't know you meant us back there. Anything we can do for you?" Frank interrupted.

"You dropped this," the man replied, holding out his hand to Daniel. In it was an old black and white photo.

"Thank you," Daniel said, taking the photo.

"It was back by the bathrooms. I know how special pictures are," said the man. "I was looking for you all night after that."

Frank noticed the innocent expression and simplicity in his speech, the limited mobility of the man upon closer inspection. The security guard was a guard in name only and didn't carry a gun. His heart went out to the man, as did Sarah's.

"That was so nice of you," she assured him, extending her hand.

"I didn't want him to miss it later on," the man said, shaking Sarah's hand.

"I appreciate it very much. Thank you, again," Daniel said, looking down at the photograph, gently rubbing his thumb over the surface.

"Well, have a good night," said the man, turning and walking away.

Frank watched the guard blend back into the crowd and night until he was no longer visible. He looked at Daniel and wondered about the photograph.

"Who's in the photo, Daniel?" Maria asked gently.

"Me, at least I think so. It's the only photo I have of myself as a child," he said looking at the reflection.

No one said anything but waited for Daniel to continue. He didn't, so Frank asked if he could take a look. Daniel handed the black and white image to him.

"I don't know who the man is with me," he added.

The photo was worn and creased, the edges frayed from lack of protection. Staring back at him was a baby, about a year old. He held a blanket and a stuffed animal. The child held a slight smile on his face, as if he'd just been crying, but was distracted by the camera. A young man was holding him and smiling at the child. Daniel might not know who the man was, but Frank did. He'd recognize Charley anywhere. He didn't share that information yet.

Frank handed the photograph back to Daniel, who carefully slid the image inside his wallet.

"I guess the picture fell out of my pocket when I took my cell phone out," he offered.

"When?" Maria asked.

"On the ramp, by the toilets," Daniel said.

"You mean the time you left us?" Frank asked.

"Yes, I think so. That's when I saw him behind me on the ramp," Daniel replied.

"Where'd you go then? I searched all over the place," Frank said.

"Into one of the port-o-potties," he smiled.

"Stayed a while, did we?" Frank drawled.

"Yes, well, only to hide from the security guy," Daniel said, glancing at Maria and blushing.

"Kind of an awful place to hide," Sarah said.

"It was and I didn't know if he'd be waiting when I got out," Daniel nodded.

"Well, it all worked out. Since I thought he'd been watching us all night, I guess I was just paranoid," Frank said.

"I was able to get a few more shots of the horse when I came out, too. No one was around," Daniel said.

They drove in the night, talking about the rodeo, the people and laughing about the experience. There were some clear shots of the horse they believed belonged to Ed Tate, but Frank had to figure out the best way to share the information with the man. After taking Maria home, the drive to their house was made in comfortable silence, no one wishing to share their thoughts aloud.

———

That night, Frank held Sarah closely in their bed. He waited to hear the steady rhythm of her soft breathing, indicating she'd finally drifted into sleep. It didn't come.

"You awake?" he asked.

"Unfortunately," she mumbled.

"I can't sleep either," he said.

"I keep thinking of that photo Daniel had," she said.

"I do, too," he replied.

"I've never seen it before. Have you?" Sarah asked.

"No, but it obviously means something to him," Frank said.

"I can't imagine not having some sort of identity. He has nothing tangible to define his past or who he was, only terrible memories," she said, nuzzling closer to her husband.

"So he holds on to a tattered photograph, as if it's priceless," Frank muttered.

"It is to him," she said.

"Sarah, I know who the man is in the picture," he said.

"Who?" Sarah asked. She lifted her face to look at him.

"Charley. I don't know why I didn't share that with Daniel. Just couldn't for some reason," Frank said.

"Well, it makes sense, doesn't it? Charley would've known Daniel from the beginning," she added.

"Yes, but something about the way Charley was looking at Daniel," he sighed into her hair.

"What do you mean?" Sarah asked.

"It suddenly hit me when I saw the photo. What if Charley is Daniel's father?" he blurted.

"No, it couldn't be. How could he let his child live that way?" she asked.

"I don't know, but I'm going to find out," Frank said.

"How? He might not know, if it's even true," she cried.

"How could he not know, Sarah? Or even suspect? If he was having sex with that shrew, he had to wonder," Frank said, a little too loudly.

"We don't know if he was having sex with her. You can't just assume it," she said.

"Charley carried a torch for the woman for years. I never understood why, but he did," Frank said.

"Do you think Daniel looks like Charley?" she asked.

"No, I don't. Charley had red hair. Probably gray now. I haven't seen him in years. And he was fair and covered with freckles," Frank said, adding, "He must've aged enough that Daniel wouldn't recognize him, either, I guess."

"I wonder what his mother looked like," Sarah mused.

"According to Charley back in the day, she was blonde and beautiful," he said.

"Sounds like Daniel favors her then," Sarah said.

"Maybe in looks, but not in personality," Frank replied.

"Frank," Sarah began, "what difference does all of this make?"

"Because I want him to be our son," he said.

"He is. Already," she assured him. "And it's just a matter of us making everything legal, that's all. He's an adult. He chose us as much as we chose him."

Frank nodded, hugging her to him. Sarah was right but something in the pit of his stomach told him his guess about Charley was true. Would it really matter? Charley waited until Daniel was fifteen years old to help him. And he sent him to them. The Charley he knew would want to be part of his son's life.

He forced himself to close his eyes. It was nearly three a.m. and in a couple of hours he'd be facing more work in the hay fields. He was tired and wanted a vacation. Maybe he'd dream of the day he and Sarah could retire, turning everything over to their son.

CHAPTER FIFTEEN

"You doing okay?" Daniel asked.

"As long as I don't fall," Joe said.

They were in the riding arena and Joe was astride Ben, one of the oldest and gentlest geldings at the ranch. Ben had been used as a lesson horse for beginners prior to coming to them. When his previous owner could no longer care for him, Frank bought the horse, basically to use for people who visited them and didn't ride much. He'd been trained well and rarely spooked. Joe and Ben got along nicely.

Daniel had worked in a number of riding lessons for Joe, always scheduled around Bill and Inez being away from the ranch, which wasn't easy. Joe had been hesitant at first, saddling Ben then refusing to get on the horse. It wasn't until the third lesson that Joe took a deep breath and said that he was ready.

And now Daniel watched as he rode Ben in a slow trot around the arena. Each lesson Joe looked a little more comfortable in the saddle. He sat up tall and held the reigns in front of him, his helmet strapped securely under his chin. Daniel thought he'd put up a fuss about wearing the helmet, but Joe was more than willing to wear it. The helmet was as much a part of the tack as the saddle and bridle to Joe. He wouldn't get on the horse without it.

"You're doing a great job, Joe," Daniel encouraged.

"You think so?" Joe asked.

"I do. Just think where you were before. You've come a long way," Daniel replied.

"I've got a long way to go," he said.

"One step at a time. There's no hurry," Daniel said.

"I just don't want to be afraid," Joe said.

"Well, I think you're losing the fear or you wouldn't be riding old Ben right now," said Daniel.

"Old Ben wouldn't hurt a fly that gets in his eye," Joe said.

"He's still a twelve hundred pound animal, Joe. You have to always take care," Daniel reminded him.

"Thanks for reminding me that he could squash me if he wanted to," said Joe.

"Ha, no, he likes you I think," said Daniel.

"No, I think old Ben tolerates me so he'll get to eat hay later," Joe laughed, reaching down to stroke the gelding's neck.

"They all do that," laughed Daniel.

"So, you and Maria are pretty serious," said Joe, changing the subject.

"Well, I am and I think she is, too," Daniel said, smiling.

"So I disappear for a while and poof you're in love with my cousin," Joe said.

"Sorry, Joe, I knew it wouldn't work between you and me," Daniel teased.

"You know what I mean," Joe began, "you haven't known each other that long."

"What? Are you going to lecture me?" Daniel asked.

"No, I'm not the 'rents. But when did the boyfriend-girlfriend thing even begin?" asked Joe.

"I don't know," Daniel said, raising his shoulders for emphasis.

"But you didn't deny it," Joe said.

"Deny what?" asked Daniel.

"That you love her. Just a minute ago when I said it," Joe said.

"No, I guess you're right. I don't deny it," Daniel said softly.

"Some serious stuff," Joe mumbled.

"Hey," Daniel began, his turn at changing the subject, "you know at some point you have to tell your parents about riding."

"I'm putting it off as long as I can," he said.

"Bill could walk around that corner any minute," Daniel said, pointing behind him.

"Well, he hasn't yet," said Joe.

"It's going to happen. Don't you think it'd be easier on them if you told them before they saw it?" Daniel asked.

"Now who's lecturing?" Joe asked.

They continued to argue good-naturedly. Daniel watched while Joe picked up the pace slightly on Ben. Joe crossed the arena and turned Ben easily in one direction and then the other. The horse willingly followed every command, stopping when asked and trotting when given a little squeeze. Joe was building his confidence by the minute. Ben was the perfect horse for Joe.

Daniel thought of Maria and what he'd admitted to Joe. Was he in love? He knew how he felt when he was around her. He thought of her all the time and his heart felt full in his chest. He imagined summer ending when she'd go away to school and it made his full heart sink. Plus, it hurt. How was he going to handle it?

The idea of not being able to see her made him wonder about his own future. He'd been thinking of school more and more. Should he try following Maria? He didn't want to leave the Carpenters because he'd finally found a home. Maybe he was afraid if he did leave, he wouldn't have a home when he returned. Deep inside he knew that wouldn't happen but it was a fear for him. But more than anything, he'd finally found the parents he had wanted all of his life. It would be too hard to leave something like that and he'd never turn his back on them. Never.

James Tate sat in his car, watching. He was waiting, too. He needed to know the exact comings and goings of those on the Carpenter ranch to gauge the best time to strike. Money was driving him now, the desire to gamble for it and the need to pay off debt because of it. Now he sat on the road watching the open gate to Frank Carpenter's property, assured that the answer to his problems rests behind the forbidden entrance for his choosing.

He had sold two more of his father's horses. It wasn't something he'd wanted to do but desperation drove a person to act in strange ways. His father was willing to lay all the blame at Frank Carpenter's feet. He had to take advantage of that weakness in Ed Tate's character.

But stealing from his father was getting risky. James thought he'd made a mistake in selling the gelding. He'd seen it in his father's eyes, the slight hesitation in responding, the confusion when told which horses were gone. Old Ed needed little push to become enraged about the wild horse sanctuary. Heck, he'd never even questioned how his horses would've left his property. His old man just wanted to believe it. But a missing gelding hinted more of theft, a fact his father couldn't ignore.

So James had to consider other opportunities and possibilities. The Carpenters had horses and plenty of them. He'd moved beyond destroying their property simply because Daniel bugged him. He was smarter than that. James Tate wasn't about to look a gift horse in the mouth. That thought and play on words made him smile. But stealing a horse from the Carpenters wouldn't be easy and could prove impossible since the place was electronically secured. At least the sanctuary was, but he wasn't sure about the domesticated horses. Those might be a little easier to lure away than the wild ones. How the hell did he think he'd be able to get one of the wild horses anyway? He needed to think a little more clearly.

Maybe guns were the answer. He knew they owned them. Everyone he knew did. If he slipped in on foot when the gate was open, then he could find a way to get in the house and see what was there for the taking. Who knew what else he might find?

He'd only been on the Carpenter property once when his dad had bought some of the hay they grew. That was all it took to know it was the most pristine and beautiful pieces of land he'd ever seen. Streams and creeks flowed through the property providing natural irrigation opportunities for terraced fields and pastures. It held several lakes and one side backed up to the National Forest. The meadows offered clusters and thickets of aspens, cottonwoods and ponderosa pines, surrounded with endless sagebrush and piñon pines. It was no wonder Ed Tate burned with jealousy for the place.

It was also the perfect location for wild horses to roam. Frank Carpenter had spared no expense in protecting these animals and they weren't easy to get to unless you were accessing the sanctuary land from the Carpenters' main house area. James had faced a heck of a time getting to an area of the sanctuary fencing to throw that barbed wire over. Using gloves, he'd stood on the bed of his truck one night, tossing various lengths of wire, careful not to injure himself in the process. And since he hadn't been able to throw wire that far, he wasn't sure if it would serve any purpose. But it made him feel better for some reason. If just one horse encountered it in any way, it would've been worth the trouble in James' malicious mind. And regardless of how his father wished to believe, James knew there was no way that those horses escaped from the Carpenter land.

However, now James was only concerned with self-preservation. Whatever the Carpenters had, he was going to take. He had to cover the debts he was facing now and consider future ones he knew would be part of his life. It was a sickness he couldn't control and he had no one to go to. His father wasn't the answer. The irony that Daniel was his only hope nearly made him laugh, but James would never let the son of a bitch know it. Stealing was his revenge now.

CHAPTER SIXTEEN

Frank, Daniel and Walt drove in silence. Armed with evidence for Ed Tate to see, Frank was dreading the encounter he knew would end badly. While helping to prove he'd had nothing to do with the disappearance of Ed's horses, shocking the man with news that his son had stolen from him wasn't going to sit well and could make things worse.

They made their way up the long drive to the Tate property. The heat bore down and full summer made the surroundings look barren and dry. Every time Frank saw Ed Tate's land, he was reminded how his own property was the exception. Color painted his land and was the result of natural water he had rights to, whereas excess water for a great number of people in the area was a scarce commodity.

Walt had called ahead, thinking it better to prepare the man they were visiting instead of ambushing him with the news. Frank wasn't sure that would make much difference but agreed to go along with Walt's decision. He was happy Daniel was with them. After the last encounter, he knew Daniel wasn't taking any chances as to what measures Ed might stoop to once they disclosed their information.

Ed Tate's round figure waited for them at the front of his house. The oversized cowboy hat he wore shielded his face from the sun but seemed to emphasize the lack of a neck on the man. Chin touching chest, his arms were crossed as if preparing for a battle. Fortunately, James Tate was nowhere in sight.

"Gentlemen," Ed nodded in greeting, as they walked up to him.

"Ed," Walt said, in response. Frank and Daniel nodded their greetings.

"Well, don't the three of you look like the kiss of death," the man said. "Better just give it to me straight."

"We have reason to believe your first mare was sold to Bain's rodeo," Walt said, clearing his throat.

"Surely you can come up with something better than that," Tate laughed, rocking back on his heels.

"Wish we could. Want to see the proof?" Frank asked.

"You better damn well believe I do," Ed replied, his eyes boring hatred into Frank's.

Walt opened an envelope and removed photos he'd had printed from Daniel's cell phone. He handed the copies to Ed. The man's face showed no emotion, but he took his time looking over all of the copies. When he refused to say anything, Walt prompted a response.

"That's your mare, isn't it Ed?" he asked.

"You know it looks like it, but I can't quite be sure now, can I?" Tate responded smugly, smacking the stack of photos against the palm of his hand.

"What do you mean? You know it's your horse," Frank retorted.

"I know it looks like my horse, but I don't know if it is," Tate challenged.

"C'mon, Ed. Admit it," Walt said.

"Admit what?" he asked.

"That you made a hell of a mistake, that's what, for starters," Frank nearly yelled.

"Here's what I don't get," Ed began, "if this is my horse, how did it get to Bain's?"

"We said it was sold," Walt reminded him.

"You see, that doesn't make any sense, unless you sold it," Tate said accusingly, pointing the stack of photos in Frank's direction.

"You're a damn fool," Frank said, shaking his head.

"I've been called worse," Ed responded.

"I have no reason to want your horse, Ed. I've plenty of my own," Frank said.

"You have every reason to cover your tracks, though, once you discovered I'd been right all along," Tate replied.

"There's no getting through to you," Frank said.

"No need to get through to somebody when they already know the answer," the man replied stubbornly.

"Ed, we know who sold your mare and it wasn't Frank," Walt said.

"Who then? Daniel here?" Tate asked sharply, looking at Daniel suspiciously.

"Ed, you're trying my patience," Frank started.

"No," Walt said, interrupting Frank. "This is hard to say, Ed, but here it is. James sold your mare."

Ed Tate didn't have the ability to hide his emotions then. He recoiled as if he'd been slapped. Once the initial shock from Walt's statement wore from his face, rage contorted his features into an ugly mask. The man was barely able to form a coherent sentence.

"A thief? You're accusing my boy of stealing from me? His own father?" the man spewed.

"Yes, we are, Ed. Your boy is in a heap of trouble," Walt replied.

"Bullshit," Tate said, wiping his mouth. He couldn't control the spit accumulating in the corners of his lips.

"He more than likely sold your other horses, too," Frank said.

"More than likely, huh? Funny, he doesn't need the money. I've got plenty to give him, so you can take your 'more than likely' and shove it," Ed said.

"It isn't about need, Ed. He gambles. James has acquired some major debt," Walt said.

Tate's face changed then. Fury was replaced with a recollection or memory none of the men standing before him were aware of. The man looked as if he finally understood something that had been troubling him.

"Get off my property," the man said quietly.

"Just stop with this nonsense, Ed. Get on with your life," Frank said.

"Get on with my life? You come here accusing my son like this and have the audacity to tell me to get on with my life?" his voice rose.

"Where is James?" Walt asked suddenly.

"He ain't here," Tate replied.

"You need to be careful, Ed," Walt continued.

"You mean I should be afraid of my son?" he asked incredulously.

"No, of the people he is associating with," Walt said.

"Leave. Now," Tate said.

Frank, Daniel and Walt turned to make their way back to the BLM truck. Opening the doors, they were stopped by Ed Tate's warning.

"Oh, Mr. High and Mighty," he said, pointing at Frank, "the sheriff might be paying you a visit. Something about harboring a runaway. I've no idea what that could be about."

And with that, Ed Tate turned his back and walked into his house, slamming the door behind him. The finality of the sound proof that their business was finished, allowing them to leave.

They drove back to the Carpenter ranch, making small talk but never once discussing the meaning behind Ed Tate's last statement. Walt didn't inquire, but Frank knew he had to be curious about the meaning.

Frank knew with certainty that Tate had probed into Daniel's life. It didn't surprise him. As a matter of fact, he wondered why it had taken as long as it did for the man to show any interest. He and Sarah never made an effort of hiding Daniel from anyone. Charley had been able to acquire a copy of Daniel's birth certificate and sent it to them. They used it to enroll him in school and no one questioned it. Most people knew their history and lack of success with adoption, so it was basically assumed he was an orphan they were adopting. It helped that he was a good kid whom everyone liked.

He had no idea what kind of legal ramifications would come of this. Hopefully, nothing would happen, since Daniel was an adult and could attest to his past and current living conditions. Frank and Sarah could handle any of that together and had even talked about it in the past. His only worry concerned Daniel's father and what his role would be in demanding some sort of payback. His concern was for Daniel. Could their son handle facing the monster of his past?

Glancing toward the back seat, Frank saw Daniel staring out the window, lost in thought. He could only imagine what was playing in the young man's head at the moment. When they got home, he and Sarah would sit down with him. The three of them would have an honest discussion about their future and what might happen with all of this. It didn't matter what other people thought. It only mattered that Daniel could handle what might come. He and Sarah had to make certain of it. That's what families did. It's what parents are supposed to do.

———

Frank, Sarah and Daniel left district court with a feeling of relief. Something they had planned on doing was a reality. The petition to adopt Daniel had been submitted and the application for changing his surname filed. Aside from publishing a notice of the name change in the local paper, the matter was out of their hands. Neither would become legal until the requisite time had passed. Until then, all they could do was wait and hope there would be no hitches in the legal process.

They could also celebrate, which is what Sarah intended for them to do. After meeting with their lawyer to discuss changing their will, she suggested going to lunch at a new restaurant that had just opened in town.

"I want to have a party," she announced, as they sat down at a table by the front window.

"What are we celebrating, darlin'?" Frank drawled, winking at Daniel.

"Hmm, let me see," she began, smiling, "a new son, a bright future, a happy home, health, family. I could go on."

"I'm sure you could," Frank replied, leaning over and kissing her on the cheek.

Ed Tate's bombshell had pushed them into action. There had been no visits from the sheriff or, worse, Daniel's biological father, but Tate's words spurred them into making it all legal. Trouble could still come, but Sarah was relieved and happy and living in the moment. Frank wasn't going to deny her that experience.

"So who would you like to invite to this shindig?" Frank asked.

"Everybody," she replied simply, her smile wide and bright and her eyes shining.

"You think you'd want to cook for that many people?" Frank asked, smiling too. There were always little moments in their marriage when he was reminded how much he loved his wife. This was one of them.

"Oh, I don't plan on cooking. Well, maybe a little bit. I want to have it catered," she said.

"Well, now I know we're getting fancy," he said, laughing.

"Daniel, what do you think? Would you mind if we had a party?" Sarah asked.

"I don't mind. I kind of like it but what if none of it becomes legal?" he asked, his blue eyes worried.

"It will, Daniel," Sarah replied, reaching over and grabbing his hand. "It will."

"I just can't help thinking something bad is going to happen," he replied, looking down.

"Daniel, I know Ed Tate finding out about things kind of forced our hand, but this was something we'd planned on doing anyway. You're an adult. Even if your biological father contested this, given your history, I don't think there's anything that can keep it from becoming legal," Frank said.

"You heard Tate. What about harboring a runaway? What kind of trouble have I caused the two of you?" he asked, his eyes bright.

"You haven't caused the least bit of trouble, Daniel, in any way. You've brought us joy and hope," Sarah replied. "We doubt anything will come of this threat."

"Sarah's right, Daniel. You heard our lawyer. Because of the abuse, he doesn't think we really have anything to worry about," Frank tried reasoning. "Whatever comes, we'll fight it."

"But the worry. Is it worth it?" Daniel cried.

"You're our son. Yes, it's worth it," Sarah replied.

The simplicity of her response nearly moved Frank to tears. They'd been through a lot together, the two of them. The early years of making ends meet and the endless pain and disappointment of losing every child that they conceived together. He knew if anyone could get through life's hard knocks, it would be them. They'd certainly had their share. Frank knew Sarah would fight with an indescribable ferocity to protect a son she'd waited all her life to have. He'd share that fight with her.

He reached across the table and took his wife's hand in his. With his other hand, he touched Daniel's shoulder. They'd get through anything as a family.

"Could I ask a favor?" Daniel asked.

"Anything," Frank replied.

"Could we wait on having a party? Maybe in the fall when things are settled. I just don't want to jinx anything," Daniel said.

"We can have the party any time you like," Sarah assured him

"You do have a birthday coming up," Frank reminded him.

"That's right. We could have one big celebration then. How does that sound?" Sarah asked.

"Alright," Daniel replied, smiling.

"That's settled then. A big birthday family whoopla," Frank said, looking at the menu. "Anybody else ready to eat?"

"I am. I'm starving," Daniel replied.

"You're always starving," Frank teased.

"I can't deny that," laughed Daniel.

They ordered their food and talked about family things. Daniel confessed he'd thought about taking some college classes. Both Frank and Sarah were receptive to the idea. They told him the more education he had, the more opportunities he would enjoy.

All three had been enjoying the view from the front window, watching people walk and traffic pass with purpose. As they ate their food, a familiar face caught their eyes.

"Isn't that Merrill?" Sarah asked.

"It sure is," Frank replied.

They watched as Merrill crossed the street and walked half a block. He entered a jewelry store on the corner. Within five minutes, he exited the building carrying a small gift bag. In no time, a woman ran up to him and they embraced in greeting, as if they'd planned to meet.

Merrill then kept his arm around the woman's waist and they walked away together, out of sight.

"Well, I would've bet that gift from the jewelry store was meant for Maria, but now I'm not so sure," Frank said, raising his eyebrows for emphasis.

"Oh, stop," said Sarah, laughing. "We don't have a clue what that was about."

"Did you recognize the woman?" Daniel asked, thinking of Maria and wondering if he should tell her what they had seen.

"She didn't look familiar to me," Sarah replied.

"Nope, no idea," Frank said, signaling for their check.

They left the restaurant and ran errands before going home. Sarah said she was going to take advantage of having both of them free during a workday, as she rarely had the opportunity to enjoy those occasions. It was late afternoon when they reached the ranch. The horses nickered their greeting and after the day's accomplishments, Daniel felt complete, as if he finally belonged.

CHAPTER SEVENTEEN

Sarah watched as the physical therapists worked with the young rider on horseback. Physically challenged, the girl had difficulty walking without assistance. Horses are thought to have similar gaits as humans. Being on the back of a horse allowed her to experience the feeling of a normal gait through the horse. The therapists hoped this would help her develop a normal walking pattern of her own.

The smile on the girl's face was enough for Sarah to know the emotional connection between person and horse was healing. Regardless of what the child could do physically, her mind and soul also benefited from the interaction with the horse.

Sarah had driven to Albuquerque to visit the equine therapy program she learned of through a contact at the hospital. She knew they would have to start much smaller at the ranch, but seeing firsthand the benefits of the program assured her she'd made the right decision in wanting to create a therapy program.

Initially, she wanted to start therapy for special education children, with a focus on emotionally troubled youth. She hoped children from the reservation would participate and counted on Inez's help in encouraging counselors and tribal leaders to support their program.

Sarah thought of Daniel's past and how being around horses allowed him to grow and gain confidence. He was living proof of someone who came out of the darkness by interacting with the animals. She and Frank had been there for him and helped along the way, providing stability and parental guidance, but much of his confidence came from silent communication and understanding of these great creatures.

She was so happy when the adoption and change of name papers had been signed the other day. Making all of it legal had nearly left her giddy with silliness but she hadn't cared. She wanted to shout to the world that she had a son and no one could take that from her. She wanted to tell everyone she could now relate to parenting issues all of her friends talked about, the same ones that in the past had left her and Frank feeling empty. It was ridiculous, Sarah knew, but she had wanted a child for so long, the dull ache was finally replaced with hopefulness. It didn't matter that Daniel was no longer a child. He was still their son.

The possibility they might face obstacles before all of it became official was real. Ed Tate's words to Frank hung in the air and wouldn't dissipate. Legal threats involving the sheriff and potential contact from Daniel's biological father concerned them. She still worried about Ed's vendetta against her husband and what the outcome would be since James' behavior had been disclosed. Then there was Charley, Frank's old friend. Could he really be Daniel's blood father? If so, how couldn't he claim him?

But Sarah refused to let any of that spoil the simple fact that she and Frank finally had what they always wanted. She listened as the young girl on the horse laughed. It sounded as if she were trilling a song in laughter, a clear sound, sweet and innocent and honest. It came from the heart.

Sarah's eyes were bright as she watched the child. So much to overcome. Yes, she knew if these children could face life everyday, so could her family. She was determined.

———

Merrill watched his daughter take a customer's order for lunch. She flashed a smile at the older couple sitting in the booth and joked with them comfortably. Mama was smart, kind and beautiful. He was so proud of his only child and he'd missed so much of her life. But it had been necessary. He realized it now.

Stuck in the old ways was how his ex-wife had described him. And he had been. But that was their culture and unless you moved away from it, you were forced to live it, whether you accepted it or not.

So his ex took the child away for a better life. He had wanted to stop her but he knew taking care of a young child wasn't something he could've done on his own. And once they were gone, Merrill embraced reclusiveness and retreated further into the ways of his Navajo ancestors.

Sweat lodge purifications became part of his life. Rituals at the home of his grandmother, who lived in a dirt-floored hogan, were commonplace until she died in her home and the hogan was left abandoned. The rest of his family had adopted more modern homes, but still practiced the ways he had come to enjoy. His culture was important to him. He thought it could sustain him the rest of his life until he met Sandra.

She came into his life one night when he was about to close the bar. It was winter and the snow was coming down hard. He remembered he couldn't wait to get home and pass the cold night in the comfort of his house. When he'd heard the door open to his place, he was behind the bar and was about to call out that they were closed. But something had caused him to look up first. She was standing in the doorway, shivering and wearing a thin coat that was unbuttoned. Her hair was plastered to her head from the wetness and the look of hopelessness on her face disturbed him.

He immediately got her to sit down and made a fresh pot of coffee, hoping that would warm her. Eventually it did and he learned she lived on the reservation. She'd just come from the hospital with her husband. He had suffered a stroke and she wasn't sure he was going to make it. They talked a long time that night and when it was time for her to go, he offered to drive her home in the storm, but she said she was used to driving in that kind of weather. Plus, she didn't live far.

Sandra's husband survived but with a severe disability. She devoted the next two years to caring for him, occasionally coming in to the bar to say hello to Merrill when she'd get a short break. Their friendship grew but her devotion to her husband never wavered. Merrill wished he could help in some way and offered many times, but Sandra always declined.

About eight months ago Merrill heard Sandra's husband had died. He didn't see her for a long time and he wondered if he ever would again. Then out of the blue, she showed up one night at the bar. She looked healthy and rested and wore a smile on her face that only appeared briefly during the past two years. But the smile lingered longer, almost shyly, and he realized he'd missed her.

They started seeing each other, quietly and privately. She felt guilt at betraying her husband's memory. He felt guilt for no reason at all. Maybe it was because he'd convinced himself that his culture was enough, but found out it wasn't. And when the two of them were apart, Merrill was miserable. Sandra said she was, too. Still, they were careful and Merrill hadn't shared the news of Sandra with Maria. He knew he had to. He wanted to, but he felt hypocritical for some reason. His ex-wife had moved on and remarried. Why didn't he feel he deserved to do the same?

"Daydreaming again, Papa?" came Maria's teasing voice, as she walked past him.

"You know me too well, little girl," he smiled.

His daughter smiled at him as she walked past, greeting another group of customers who sat at one of her tables. He had enjoyed her visit with him these last few months and appreciated the help she provided at the restaurant. Both she and Joe were always willing to help out whenever they could. It would be quiet again in the fall, when Maria left for college and Joe would return to school. He'd continue getting Joe's help on the weekends but he'd miss seeing his daughter.

Merrill had been happy to hear Maria was still going to school. Her relationship with Daniel worried him to the point that he felt she'd change her mind just to stay here with him. He was a good kid, that Daniel, Merrill thought. But he wanted the best for his little girl and that started with an education. Smiling to himself, he thought it ironic that he sounded just like his ex-wife had when she left. She had wanted the best for Maria, too, and left him. Maybe he should open his eyes to the world a bit more.

He would need to share the role Sandra played in his life with his daughter before she left for school. That was only fair to both women. And wasn't it fair to him, too? If he and Sandra could be open with their relationship, perhaps he could move on with life and learn that it was okay to be happy.

Picking up the telephone, he dialed Sandra's number. He was going to ask to see her and ask if she'd meet Maria. It was time the two most important people in his life met each other. He watched his daughter as he spoke to Sandra and for once he felt good about the future.

CHAPTER EIGHTEEN

Frank walked from the building he'd constructed to house their bales of hay. A couple of deliveries were being made today and some of his local customers were picking up their own. They usually didn't deliver the hay unless it was a big order or one out of state. Then Frank hired a fellow he knew to make the deliveries. He didn't have the transportation means or the time to deliver those large orders. Most of the ranchers he knew who bought from them were able to transport their own hay, but Frank was always willing to do a favor by delivering smaller orders to those who needed it.

The days had been kind and clear during this hay season. They'd been able to mow the most recent cutting with ease and the drying-out process went smoothly, with no threat of rain. Once it had dried and was raked, it seemed to take no time for their small square baler to finish the job, allowing the Bale Bandit to bundle twenty-one small bales of hay together, secured by metal bands. Frank marveled at the efficiency of the equipment. He was always tired at the end of the day from the physical labor but wondered how hard of a job hay farming would have been without the modern conveniences.

He was proud of the hay they grew. Alfalfa was nutritious for horses and livestock and his customers appreciated the quality he provided. He remembered the day he'd approached his former boss about growing their own hay. It was as if a light had turned on in the man's head. He'd eagerly allowed Frank to take charge and it had been a learning process along the way, from seed selection, soil preparation and weed control to learning the exact time to cut. Then you did a lot of praying and hoping there'd be no rain during the drying out process. Sometimes the gods had listened, and other times a deaf ear was turned to all of their pleas, as the skies opened and dropped buckets of rain, sometimes ruining the crops.

But Frank finally got it right. Trial and error combined with elevated and well-drained land allowed him a successful crop of alfalfa in an area where it isn't often grown. While he didn't know at the time that growing his own hay would ultimately feed a sanctuary of wild horses through harsh winters, Frank had always felt good about using the land in that way.

He watched his son help one of the ranchers load some bales onto his truck bed. His son. The words still caught in his chest as if to remind him never to take it for granted. Not yet legal, but Frank didn't need the papers to prove anything. Somehow Daniel had been his son from the moment he first stepped foot on the ranch. He walked over to help them finish.

"Always happy with your hay, Frank," Mr. Turner, the rancher, said.

"Glad to hear it," Frank replied.

"You, Sarah and Daniel here are always welcome out at the house for supper anytime," Turner said.

"Well, I appreciate the invitation. Just let us know when," Frank grinned.

"You know Millie. She's always reminding me to invite you all and I keep forgetting," the man laughed.

"Maybe you should just tell Millie to call Sarah and set a time. I know if Sarah didn't plan things, we'd never get anything done," Frank said.

The man Turner laughed at that, nodding that it was the same for him. If it weren't for his wife, he would probably forget to eat and get a haircut he'd said. Frank and Daniel exchanged smiles, knowing that was probably the truth. Turner was an absent-minded man whose wife worried over every move the man made or didn't make. She treated him like a young child and he often acted like one.

"Hey, did you hear the news about Ed Tate's good-for-nothin' son?" Turner asked.

"What news is that?" Frank asked cautiously, glancing at Daniel.

"Oh, that he'd gotten into some trouble with gambling," the man replied.

"Well, we'd heard some rumblings," Frank said.

"Seems the kid stole some of Ed's horses and then disappeared," Turner said.

"What do you mean disappeared?" asked Daniel.

"That he ran away or something. Been missing for a couple of days," the man replied.

"We hadn't heard about that," Frank said.

"I guess the sheriff came calling and it scared him off," Turner said.

"Anyone know where he could be?" Frank asked.

"I heard some believe he left the state, but you know how people talk," the man replied.

"What about Ed? How's he taking it?" Frank asked, already knowing the answer.

"Pissed off. Same old Ed, blaming everyone else. You know how it is," Turner said.

"Yeah, I do," mumbled Frank.

"Well, I better get going. Wouldn't want Millie to send a search party out for me," laughed the man.

"You take care and thank you," Frank said.

"Sure thing. Always appreciate it, Frank," Turner said, closing the door to his truck.

Frank and Daniel watched as the man drove away with the bales of hay. Frank knew Turner had already forgotten about mentioning the supper invitation to them. Smiling, he turned to Daniel.

"You've done a good job, Daniel. With the hay this season and the horses. It hasn't been easy," Frank said.

"Everybody's worked hard," came the reply.

"I know and I appreciate everyone's efforts. But the sanctuary seems to be your calling," said Frank.

"It just feels right. It doesn't even feel like work," Daniel said, smiling.

"When you're working for something you love, it doesn't feel like work, I guess," Frank replied.

"I know and I do love it here," Daniel nodded.

"So," Frank began, changing the subject, "kind of disturbing to hear about James Tate."

"Yeah, but I guess it doesn't surprise me. Seems he's capable of anything," Daniel said.

"And that worries me a bit. Any ideas as to where he could be?" Frank asked.

"No, not really. You think he could be staying with someone?" asked Daniel.

"It's possible, I guess," Frank replied.

They watched as the last of the scheduled pickups departed for the day. Something deep down worried Frank into thinking James Tate wasn't far enough away. He couldn't imagine the kid would get very far without money or help. And he had to assume James had no money because of the gambling debt he'd acquired. All of that led to desperation, which meant a person was liable to do anything to get what he thought he needed.

Frank scanned his property. He wouldn't have peace of mind until James Tate was found.

Survival skills had never been a problem for him, James thought. He hadn't become an Eagle Scout for nothing. He'd camped enough as a kid, too, so living off the land had been a snap. And living off the Carpenters' lush land was even better. Water, shade and places to lie low were plentiful. It was easy to camouflage yourself in these surroundings and possibly never be found.

And so far, it'd been easy to steal a few things of necessity, too. He watched the comings and goings of people on the ranch easily with binoculars. The Carpenters foolishly left their doors unlocked most times during the day, so he snuck in the house a couple of times, finding bread, apples and cheese for the taking, pilfering just enough that no one noticed.

In the short amount of time he'd been in the house, he looked for guns, too. James had found a locked gun cabinet in a back room. Trying to take any would alert the family to the theft and he couldn't take that chance. Not yet anyway. He'd brought a gun of his father's out of necessity, but the time would come when James would be ready to move on. He'd need the guns to sell and if he had to use them for leverage, then so be it. He wasn't above that.

His thoughts turned to the day the sheriff had visited his house. As soon as he'd seen the car come up the drive, he knew he had to bolt. Not even waiting for a summons from his old man, he'd piled enough of his belongings into a backpack and left. His father had been acting strangely anyway but wouldn't share what had been on his mind, so he suspected it had something to do with the sheriff's visit. Damn, if he'd just been able to control his habit. Now his life was ruined and he'd be damned if he went down without a fight.

He wondered if he could steal a horse, too. That nice gelding Daniel called Misfit would probably bring a pretty price from somewhere. Man, he wished he had half the horse sense Daniel possessed. He'd watched his rival work with that horse and it was as if he possessed an extra sense that allowed communication the animal understood.

It was the same with the wild horses. Daniel rode out across the sanctuary land and mingled with those damn beasts, as if he were part of their herds. Often it was mesmerizing just watching him stand in the midst of them, the horses standing as statues and watching Daniel go about his business. Then Daniel sometimes kneeled down, being very still and the horses ventured closer. He had to admit it was an amazing sight. Too bad James didn't care a lick about horses. Maybe that was his problem and the pain in the ass animals picked up on it. They were a means to an end in his opinion and were nothing but trouble.

But he would have to think of better plans soon. It was late summer and while living in the wild was fairly easy at the moment, particularly when the copse of trees provided cover from the sun and prevented discovery, late fall and winter were completely different stories. No way could he survive the brutal winters, nor would he want to. He'd freeze to death. Something must come his way, and soon.

———

Sarah brought the groceries inside. She could have sworn she'd just bought cheese and deli meat but now they were out again. She smiled, thinking of Daniel's appetite and how Frank teased him about it. More than likely they had both raided the refrigerator when she wasn't looking.

She'd received some interesting news earlier that day. A woman she met through all her dealings with the equine therapy program called with a question. Were she and Frank still interested in adopting? A four-year-old child was suddenly available and in need of a home. Both of the little girl's parents had been killed in an auto accident and there were no surviving relatives to take the child. The little girl, with physical limitations of her own, had been born with a clubfoot and wore a leg brace. She'd been having physical therapy sessions with the woman who called Sarah.

Sarah had mixed feelings. Taking the child in didn't mean instant adoption. In her heart she knew they would welcome the little girl into their home with open arms. But they'd had the carrot dangled in front of their eyes too many times in the past, only to have it yanked away by someone's change of heart. She wasn't sure she had the strength to do it again. The bond and attachment developed with the child don't end when the child leaves. She and Frank might actually have to say no, but what would become of the little girl?

"How's my favorite wife?" Frank drawled, coming through the kitchen door, drawing Sarah from her thoughts.

"You telling me you have more than one?" she asked, smiling.

"Well, you never can tell about us cowboys. We're breakin' hearts left and right," he said, pulling her close.

"Don't I know it? You better never break mine," she said, kissing his cheek.

"I would never dream of it, darlin'," he mumbled into her hair.

She held him close and drew strength from his embrace. He smelled of the outdoors, of earthiness and horses and of living. The worn collar on his shirt was soft against her face and his hands were firm on her back. She loved everything about her husband. And she told him of the phone call about the little girl while they stood in the kitchen embracing.

"What do you think?" he asked quietly. She heard his soft sigh before the question.

"I don't know what to think. We know how these things usually end," she said.

"Yes, but there's always a chance this one won't," he replied.

"You mean you'd like to think about it?" she asked, searching his face.

"I don't know what I mean, Sarah," he replied, touching her cheek.

"If we walk away from this, what happens to the child?" Sarah asked.

"Maybe someone else adopts her," he suggested.

"Or maybe she gets shuffled around from home to home, or gets lost in the system until she turns eighteen," Sarah said.

"Yes, or maybe she comes here and we give her the love and home we've always been capable of giving," Frank said.

"Sounds like you've made up your mind," she said, her eyes getting bright.

"Just agreeing with my sweet wife because I already knew she wouldn't turn a child away," he replied.

"And neither would you," she said.

"You're right, I probably wouldn't," he replied.

"Just like Daniel," Sarah quietly said.

"Yes, just like Daniel," he mumbled.

"Well, that's settled, I guess. I'll return the call and see where we go from here," she stated.

"You do that," Frank started, glancing at the bags of food on the counter, "are you planning on feeding an army?"

"No, but it seems I can't keep the food stocked around here, so I bought a little extra," she laughed.

"That's what a couple of hungry men will do," he smiled.

Sarah watched as Frank poured water from a pitcher and drank a full glass in nearly one gulp. She smiled. His habits comforted her. Soon they would fall in love with another child and she hoped the tie of love wouldn't be severed.

CHAPTER NINETEEN

Daniel sat near the old kiva. In the past this place had been his refuge, a place to clear the cobwebs of memories that regularly haunted him. But it was different now.

It had been a while since he'd endured one of his nightmares. They had fizzled into restless nights and daytime distractions. The horror and fear of waking abruptly, drenched in sweat with memories of a monster after him were gone. He knew his biological father could find him if he wanted, but he no longer feared what the man might do to him. He worried what the devil might do to Frank and Sarah.

Maybe his courage came from the fact he was an adult and wouldn't be forced to go back to a dark time in his life. It probably had more to do with the adoption process and making it legal. He'd never wanted anything from the Carpenters but a home. And he'd been given so much more. They were his parents and he loved them for it. Now the monster from his past could accuse them of a crime simply for protecting him. It made him sick to his stomach.

He reached down and gave Bob a pat on the head. The dog was lounging beside him in the grass, his eyes relaxed slits and his mouth slightly open and panting. Bob was content and happy just to be there with Daniel.

There were no wild horses in sight that day, which wasn't unusual. The times Daniel had encountered Espíritu's band were always at night. Some of the other herds might make an appearance but there were never guarantees.

Daniel had learned one thing from that last encounter with Espíritu and the mountain lion. It lay in the shape of a shotgun at his side. While he'd never admit to enjoying the use of fircarms, he recognized the need for them at times. He wasn't a great shot, but Frank had been patient enough to help him become a decent one if he had to be. If nothing else, the blast of the gun would scare whatever predator away even if he didn't hit it. It was better than nothing. That was Frank's reasoning.

Bob's sudden movement caught Daniel by surprise. Sitting abruptly, the dog's ears were alert and his nose twitched, as if trying to determine by scent what had caught his attention. A low rumble stirred in the animal's throat and his brown eyes scanned the horizon. Bob sensed something that he didn't like.

Tightening his grip on the leash, Daniel carefully glanced around and saw nothing. He decided it was time to go.

"C'mon, boy," Daniel said. Bob wouldn't budge, the dog's eyes fastened on something in the distance.

"Bob, let's go," he urged. The rumble in the dog's chest turned into a growl. Then Bob jumped on all fours and started barking, the sound fierce and direct, as if he were trying to alert Daniel to potential danger.

"What is it, boy? I don't see anything," he said, scanning the area but only viewing trees past the open pasture. Nothing looked out of the ordinary to him.

Then he heard it. Gunfire sliced through the silence and sent him and Bob scampering for the truck. Daniel only heard one shot ring out, but he wasn't waiting around for anymore. He started the truck and sped off. He had no idea who would be shooting a gun so close or why. He needed to find Frank in a hurry.

It was all James Tate could do to keep from laughing. He'd never seen Daniel move so fast in all his life. He probably shouldn't have fired that shot but he just couldn't help it. It was too tempting. His archenemy was relaxing in open view and didn't know he was being watched. If it hadn't been for the stupid dog, he probably could've put old Daniel out of his misery if he'd wanted to.

Did he just shoot Daniel in the leg, arm, chest or head? Where he shot him would determine James' fate. But what did he care? His life was screwed anyway. But the dog's barking made Daniel aware of something, so James hadn't had the time to consider his possibilities. The dog's bark had startled James so much that the shot went into the trees. Then he watched Daniel grab the dog and run for his life. It was funnier than hell.

Now it was time to move, however. His action hadn't been planned but would now cause his plans to be changed. Or at least accelerated. He'd hoped to get through the remainder of the summer before measures were taken. Oh, well. Such was life.

He picked up the backpack he'd abandoned nearby, putting his arms through the straps. Carrying his gun, he walked with purpose. James Tate knew exactly where he was headed. The Carpenter's house wouldn't be too far and hopefully he could get there before Daniel could alert his posse. They would more than likely take off for the land first without thinking of the house anyway. He smiled at his cleverness, actually. If he were lucky, the only person he might encounter would be the pretty wife. Snarling at the thought, he felt it might just be his lucky day.

———

Sarah sat at her desk, staring at the computer screen. She'd been trying to come up with an outline for the therapy program all morning, but her thoughts kept going back to the little girl who would soon be sharing their home. Sarah wanted very much to be excited, but she was determined to stay levelheaded about the whole process. It was the only way to survive and not have your heart broken.

From her office, she heard the creaking sound that the kitchen door made when opened and then the door slammed. It wasn't unusual for Frank or Daniel to come inside the house at various times throughout the day. That's why they always left the doors unlocked. When neither one of them came looking for her, she called out.

"Hey, I'm in here, working."

A few minutes passed and still not a word from her husband or son. One of them was still in the house since she hadn't heard the door creak indicating they'd gone outside.

"Frank? Daniel? You there?" she called, casually, typing on the keyboard.

There was still no answer. Sarah turned slightly in her chair, looking toward the door. She listened, but there was no sound. Something didn't seem right. Pinpoint goosebumps appeared on her arms, a physical indication of the strong premonition she was getting. Frank and Daniel would have responded to her. Someone else was in the house and didn't wish to reply.

Slowly, she rose from her chair. With as much care as possible, she crossed the room to the door. The house was old and the floors indicated when weight shifted across them. She knew the wood planks suggested her progress, however the same couldn't be said for the trespasser. No sound had been made since she'd heard the door creak. Had she been mistaken and Frank or Daniel opened the door, but changed their mind, staying outdoors? Or was the intruder waiting to surprise her?

She quietly slid a brass bookend from a shelf by the door, intending to use it if necessary. It wouldn't do her much good if the surprise guest had a gun, but she'd sure give him one heck of a headache to remember her by.

Sarah stepped into the hallway. She could hear the rhythmic ticking of the grandfather clock from the entryway. Its steady tapping filled the hall and every crevice of the old house, and it announced the new hour, every hour, with chimes that echoed throughout their home, sometimes so loudly it scared you if you weren't expecting it. She had inherited the antique from her grandmother and Frank complained about it incessantly because of the noise level it produced. But it was sentimental for her and he didn't do anything more than grumble about it. She didn't know how close they were to the top of the hour, but maybe the chimes would startle the intruder into leaving.

She tiptoed down the hall. It seemed like eons since she'd first heard the door creak and slam. She wanted to call out again, just in case she hadn't been heard, but she dared not. Her initial instinct had been to go to the kitchen, but her gut told her the intruder was waiting for her there. So she instantly had a change of plans. She had to get out of the house without going to the kitchen and to do that, she either had to backtrack to her office and climb out a window, or get to the front door and make a run for it. All other exits were through the kitchen: backdoor, screened porch and mudroom. It occurred to Sarah that the house could've been designed better for emergency exiting.

She decided on the front door. Gripping the bookend tightly in her right hand, she turned and walked quietly but with purpose. Fear kept the goosebumps in place and the hair at the nape of her neck on end. Perspiration dampened her skin, but her eyes focused on the big door getting closer with each step. Almost there and she'd throw it open and run like hell to find her husband. She didn't care if she looked the part of a mad woman as she went barreling from the house. Safety was her primary concern.

One more step and she reached out with her left hand to grasp the doorknob. She was almost free when she heard with horror someone standing behind her.

"Aw, now, just where do you think you're going?" came the male voice.

The voice sounded familiar to Sarah but she couldn't quite place it. Saying nothing and not turning around, she waited for the intruder's instructions. The bookend felt heavy in her hand.

"Turn around real slow," he said.

As she did, Sarah stared James Tate in the eyes. He was filthy and he smelled, his face was smudged and his clothing camouflaged. And he pointed a gun straight at her.

"Now that I have your attention, I need you to do exactly as I say," he said levelly.

She nodded, hearing her heart pound in her chest. She wondered what would happen if Frank or Daniel walked in at that moment. Panic gripped her at the thought of either of them being shot. She had to do as James said, as quickly as possible, to get him out of the house.

"I know you have that nice gun cabinet in the back room. I want you to unlock it for me. Now," he said.

As she started to move, he added, "Oh, and put that sweet bookend down right there. Wouldn't want anyone to get hurt, now would we?"

She did as he said and led him down the hall. They reached the back room that was nothing more than an oversized closet. She and Frank had decided the room was too small to make anything of it, so it became their catch-all room, including the perfect place to store Frank's guns. Daniel jokingly referred to it as the Weapon Room. Frank thought by putting the guns there, they wouldn't easily be found by an intruder. Somehow James Tate had discovered their hiding place.

"Now, unlock the cabinet," he instructed.

She went to the shelf on the far wall and picked up a music box. It was one Frank had won for her at the state fair when they were in college. Chipped from age, it still played a lullaby when opened. Removing the lid, she pulled out the set of keys hidden inside and opened the cabinet. She stepped aside, facing him.

"And just to be safe, turn around," he ordered. When Sarah hesitated, James' voice rose, "if you value your life, you'd better do as I say. I won't hesitate to kill you."

Nodding, she turned and gave her back to him. He grabbed her arms and tied her wrists together. The rope was so tight, it cut her skin but she said nothing.

"There now. Wouldn't want you to get any ideas. When I've finished here, I want you to get your car keys. You and I are goin' for a little ride," he laughed.

Sarah had to think of something to get him out of the house. Frank and Daniel could come in any minute, unprotected and unannounced. James Tate was unhinged and wouldn't hesitate to shoot either one of them if they startled him. She didn't know what to do but she'd never let either one of them get ambushed.

"You know anyone could come in and find you here," she suggested.

"Not to worry. That's why I've got these here," he said, indicating the guns.

"But you don't want to be caught, do you?" she asked.

"Why, if I didn't know better, I'd think you cared," he said sarcastically.

"I don't want to see anyone hurt," she said.

"Don't plan on hurting anybody. But plans can change," he said, shrugging his shoulders.

Sarah thought he acted as if taking a life was nothing more than changing your mind about the type of meal you wanted to eat. What had caused this young man to give up on everything and value nothing? His eyes were cold and his face held no emotion. Life, including his own, didn't mean anything to him.

"I'm sure your father is worried sick about you," she suggested.

"You're sure of that? All my old man worries about is figuring out ways to get back at your husband," James snarled.

"He must care about you, James," she said.

"Nope," he replied.

"I can't believe that," she started, but he cut her off.

"You calling me a liar?" he asked sharply, turning to look at her and raising the gun.

"No, no. I just meant a father should love his son, that's all," she said.

"Come to think of it," he began, " I bet if I shot old Frank, that would make my good daddy happy. At least, temporarily."

"No, please," she begged.

"No? Now what might you do for me so I might change my mind?" he asked, trailing a finger down the side of her neck to the opening of her blouse. His stench was nauseating and Sarah thought she might be sick.

In an instant, the grandfather clock announced the top of the hour. Loud and echoing, the chimes began and the sound startled

James. He turned and something hit the arm that held the gun, knocking it to the floor and discharging. The sound was loud inside the room and Sarah hit the floor.

"What the hell?" James Tate yelled, turning to face his attacker.

Joe stood in the doorway, fists clenched and ready to lunge. His face reflected the rage of being Tate's victim and fear for what might happen to Sarah Carpenter.

"Well, if it isn't the little Indian again. Come back for more?" James asked, pushing up his sleeves.

"No, just to finish what you started," replied Joe. And he took a swing that hit James in the nose and sent him sprawling across the room.

Startled at the action, James reached up and touched his bloody nose. His face reflected disbelief at what just happened. Then it registered rage and he jumped up, throwing his body into Joe's. Both went down with arms swinging. Punches were thrown and legs kicked, even Sarah's screams for them to stop didn't end it. Finally, Joe ended up on top of James', twisting his adversary onto his stomach. He reached for the extra rope James had used to tie Sarah's wrists and did the same to James.

Frank, Daniel and Bill rushed into the house at that point. A siren wailed in the background. All three were greeted by the sight of Joe tying James up and Sarah on the floor, huddled in the corner of the room.

"My god, Sarah," Frank said, rushing to his wife. He cut the ropes that bound her hands. Her wrists were red from the rope burns and bloody, as she'd tried to free herself. She threw her arms around her husband and he rocked her back and forth, stroking her hair and holding her tightly. Frank nodded at Daniel's worried face that she was all right.

"Are you okay, Joe?" Daniel asked then, as Bill tried to help his son up from the floor. Physically, he didn't look too bad. His lip was cut and his shirt torn, but it didn't compare to what he'd endured during his first encounter with James.

"I'm all right," Joe replied. Daniel knew from the look on his friend's face he was okay. "What about you, Mrs. Carpenter?"

"I'm fine, Joe. And thank you. I don't know what would've happened if you hadn't shown up," she said.

"And what about me?" James Tate wailed from the floor. "You think you can get away with this, you little jerk?" He spat at Joe's feet.

"I didn't get away with anything," Joe said. "And you didn't either."

The sheriff and his deputy made their way inside the house, guns drawn. After Frank assured them everything was under control, they put their weapons away and lifted James to his feet. As the deputy started to lead him outside, James' temper got the better of him.

"Just wait 'til my old man hears about this. He'll have your badge," he raged.

"After what you've done to your daddy, son, it wouldn't surprise me if he let you stew in jail for a while," the sheriff said. "Make sure you read him his rights," he added to the deputy.

The deputy nodded and led James away. Turning toward everyone else in the room, the sheriff asked what had happened. Sarah explained everything from the point when she'd first heard James enter the house. Her voice shook when she spoke of having the gun pointed at her and what James had threatened to do. Frank's face drained of color.

"Did he hurt you?" Frank asked, his voice reflecting dread at what he might hear.

"No," Sarah responded, "I was more worried about you or Daniel walking into a trap and getting shot. I just wanted to get him out of the house."

Frank nodded, holding her close. He knew if he'd walked in alone and witnessed James Tate hurting Sarah, his first instinct would've been to kill the punk. There would have been no one there who could have stopped him.

"So, Joe, how did you come about being in the house?" the sheriff asked him.

"I came over hoping to have another horseback riding lesson," Joe said sheepishly, glancing at Bill. "It was then I noticed James lurking outside the house. I saw him enter the kitchen and knew something bad was up. I tried watching some from the windows and eventually just went on in when I couldn't see anything more."

"I didn't hear you come in," Sarah said suddenly.

"I knew that screened door creaked pretty badly," Joe grinned. "It helps being small enough to crawl through the kitchen window."

"I'd say you were a hero today, Joe," the sheriff said.

Nodding, Frank went to Joe and extended his hand. Taking it, the two of them shook hands and Frank pulled him closer, and slapped him on the back. "Thank you," he said.

Turning toward the sheriff, Frank said, "I assume it was James that Daniel heard fire the gun. Once Daniel found me, we headed toward the pastures thinking he'd still be outside somewhere. I didn't even think he'd come to the house."

"You think he was aiming at you?" the sheriff asked Daniel.

"Maybe. It was so close that all I could think of doing was grabbing the dog and getting out of there," he replied.

"We might not even have come to the house if we hadn't heard the second gunshot," Frank mused, still stunned at what could have happened.

"Well, it seems you did the right thing," the sheriff said, patting him on the back. "I guess that's all I need for now, unless there's something else you all think I need to know."

"I have something," Joe said unexpectedly. "If I wanted to press charges for something how would I go about it?"

"I'd first say it was about time. Then I would say come talk to me. Bill, bring him over later, will you?" the sheriff asked.

Nodding, Bill looked at Joe and smiled. The man was proud of his son. "I'm sorry I didn't tell you about the horseback riding lessons," Joe said to him.

"You didn't need to. I already knew," Bill replied, grinning.

"How?" Joe asked.

"Maybe I'll explain it to you someday. When you have kids," he added, putting his arm on his son's shoulders. They started to leave and Sarah stopped them.

"I want to thank you, again. You were very brave today, Joe. And you're doing the right thing," she said, putting her arms around him and hugging him tightly.

"I'm just glad you're okay," he said, nodding.

Bill guided Joe toward the door, to leave for home. Daniel gave his friend a pat on the back and a thumbs-up sign before they left.

The sheriff turned toward Frank. "Just to give you a heads-up. There might be a little more trouble coming your way soon. Hope not, but it's likely. Talked to a friend of yours named Charley Thomas the other day. He explained some things to me. I think you and Sarah have done a good thing here," he said, nodding toward Daniel. "Keep me informed if trouble shows up at your door."

With that, the sheriff placed his cowboy hat on top of his head and left. Frank took his wife's hands in his and once again noticed the rope burns on her skin. Anger seethed to the surface, threatening to boil over and make him lose control at something that was no longer a threat to them. He had to take deep breaths to calm himself. A new threat loomed for them.

Their focus would be worrying if Daniel's past would reemerge and how it would affect their lives. They would face it together.

CHAPTER TWENTY

Charley's heart raced. He had to get to the airport in a hurry or he'd miss his flight to Albuquerque. The storm had traffic backed up for miles and it was bumper to bumper and nothing but brake lights in sight. Damn it! He laid on his horn when another car cut him off with inches to spare.

What a forty-eight hours it had been. Two days ago, he'd received a telephone call out of the blue from a New Mexico sheriff asking about Daniel. He instantly became alarmed, thinking something tragic had happened to him. When the sheriff assured him Daniel was well, Charley immediately became suspicious.

Then the whole story spilled. The sheriff informed him that a private investigator had snooped into Daniel's past and Charley's name had come up in the investigation. The person who hired the investigator took all he'd found to the sheriff. It was the sheriff's turn to verify what he'd been made aware of.

So Charley laid it all out for him. Everything. Daniel's life and what he'd lived through were relayed to the man over the telephone, along with Charley's role in helping him leave it behind and find Frank and Sarah Carpenter. He provided a history for the sheriff that he'd never shared with anyone. Now everything he'd felt good about the last three years was threatened because of some busybody with an ax to grind.

To make matters worse, the sheriff informed Charley that Daniel's bastard of a father had been notified and told where Daniel was living, not by the sheriff but by the investigator. Charley then found out that the one man Daniel no longer wished to see was on his way to New Mexico. How he was getting there was a mystery to Charley, because the man was rarely cognizant of his surroundings and could hardly walk, his body wasted to nothing from alcohol and cancer.

So Charley had to get to New Mexico. He'd called Frank earlier and left a message that he was on his way, that he would explain when he got there. He meant to warn his friend of Daniel's father but forgot. He tried to call back but his cell wouldn't make the connection. He figured he would try again before he boarded the plane, that is if he ever got to the airport.

Charley cursed. The rain was coming down in sheets and it was difficult to see. Brake lights had become a blur through the downpour. Several cars were pulling to the side of the road, hoping to ride out the storm until it cleared. He thought of doing the same but urgency drove him on. Hell, the flight was probably delayed, if not cancelled, he thought rationally, so why not pull over? But he inched forward in his little car, determined to make it through the torrent of rain spilling from the sky.

There was something else Charley discovered from the sheriff. Apparently, the Carpenters were legally adopting Daniel. It was just a formality, since Daniel was an adult, but the words stung Charley's soul. He should be happy that all had worked out so well that an adoption was the result, but Frank could've at least shared that information with him.

And just what would he have done with that knowledge, he asked himself? About the same thing he'd always done. Nothing. He had been nothing but a coward all of his life, but particularly so with Daniel. There were times he could hardly live with himself for it. But the shame his lifestyle brought him prevented any intervention.

Stella had been someone he hung onto for a chance at normalcy. She was beautiful and conceited and probably one of the most selfish women he'd ever met. Yet his attraction to her was something he'd never experienced. It and she gave him hope. Maybe he could love a woman after all.

They met at a coffee house by chance one morning over twenty-three years ago. It was a small place where customers seated themselves, and waitresses yelled for their orders from the counter. Charley had grabbed the only empty table he'd seen when he got there. It so happened that Stella emerged from the ladies' room and slid in the booth just as he sat down. They both claimed it as their own.

At first he didn't know what to do. A gentleman would let the woman have the table, but damn it, he was tired and hungry. And the place was packed. Then he looked intently at the woman's face and it took his breath away. The bluest eyes he'd ever seen stared at him from across the table and he couldn't find his voice. Blonde and fair, her complexion was milky, her cheekbones high. Charley later thought she knew exactly the effect she was having on him because it happened with all men who were around her. Stella was well practiced in the art of seduction and in getting her way. And he remembered that Daniel resembled her quite a bit physically as he grew older.

"Well, now, I guess we have a little problem," she'd said to him, across from the table. She wore a little pout on her lips and her eyes danced as she pushed a strand of hair behind her ear. Stella was flirting with him and it made Charley feel good.

"Now, why would it be a problem?" he'd braved asking.

"One table, two people who don't know each other," she breathed.

"Do you ever share?" he asked.

"Only if I need to," she laughed.

"Well, I guess you'll have to now if you want to eat," he said, leaning back and crossing his arms.

"So assertive! You don't look the type," she drawled, speaking with a southern lilt.

"Types go out the window when a man is hungry," Charley said.

"Oh, is that all it is?" she asked, batting her eyelashes.

"That's it," he assured her.

He then ordered coffee and two breakfast plate specials for both of them. They sat and ate, talking comfortably as if they'd known each other for years. She worked in retail and hated her job, saying she wanted more out of life. Her goal in life was to find her knight in shining armor and live happily ever after. Charley remembered her laughing when she said it, but he half thought she was serious. How unfortunate the man she chose didn't even come close.

They stayed in contact after that morning, often sharing meals and going to the movies. She relied on him to listen to her dreams, fix the problems he could and reassure her that all would be well. But she only took, never offering the same support to him. Charley didn't mind the one-sided relationship really, because he felt he was using her for his own means as well. She just didn't realize it, at least not at first.

Charley liked the sex, too. It was different with Stella. He didn't mind the affection or even lingering and talking afterwards. It seemed pretty natural with her whereas he'd been repulsed by the other women he'd had flings with. His feelings with Stella gave him hope that his inner thoughts weren't a reflection of who he really was.

Those private demons contrasted greatly with his upbringing. Raised strictly in a military family, he lived his life by the clock and the calendar. Emotions were rarely expressed and males and females never strayed from the stereotypical roles expected of them. There would be no acceptance of Charley as he really was, and that never allowed Charley to accept himself.

So finding Stella made him appear as a man should to the world. He could be someone he wasn't and half believe it when she needed him. But as their relationship progressed, he noticed subtle changes to her personality. She became erratic and irrational, often acting impulsively and doing things for shock value.

When she demanded Charley marry her, he couldn't. He tried to convince her they should wait but she wouldn't hear it. His rejection sent her spiraling into a manic mode, causing her to meet and impulsively marry a man known for his quick temper and love for alcohol.

Carl was a young hellion. Rumor had it he was the product of an abusive home and he followed the ways he was taught, learned or both. He became possessive and obsessive over Stella after they married, rarely letting her out of his sight. When he suspected she'd sneaked around on him, even when she hadn't, she paid the price for his insecurity. Too often, she met Charley wearing dark eyeglasses over bruised cheeks or black eyes.

Many times Charley tried to get her to divorce him but she wouldn't listen. Instead, she chose to chastise Charley for refusing to marry her, as if he were the one in despair, not her. It was her mental illness, Charley rationalized, but he also knew she carried a spiteful and proud streak that would never allow her to admit she'd made a mistake.

And God help him, he continued to have sex with her. He didn't love Stella in the traditional sense. He loved the idea of what might have been between them if he'd been different. She continued to give him the reprieve he needed to get through tough days. He guessed she was his best friend, while he was probably her only friend.

Shortly after discovering her pregnancy, Stella wanted to end all contact with Charley. She said things were different with a baby on the way. He wanted to know if the kid was his. She just smiled, as if she were keeping a secret, kissed him on the cheek and left. He let her go and didn't follow. He felt ashamed for it.

Charley didn't see Stella again until Daniel was almost a year old. They had met in the park and she had the baby with her. He remembered staring at the child, trying to recognize any physical similarities, but thought all babies looked alike. Again, he asked Stella for the truth and she just laughed at him.

"Here, hold him, while I get a photo," she said, handing the child to him.

"I don't know how to hold a baby," he said, awkwardly propping Daniel at his side.

"There's nothing to it," she replied, snapping pictures of Charley with baby Daniel in his arms.

They spent the rest of the afternoon together in the park, just the three of them. Charley thought Stella seemed happy, laughing freely and playing with the baby. She doted over the child and coddled him, covering him with his blanket even though there was no chill in the air. He thought motherhood was right for Stella until they were getting ready to say their goodbyes.

When she didn't think Charley was looking, Stella reached under Daniel's blanket and pinched the sleeping child's leg hard enough to wake him into a crying fit. She quickly wrapped him again and pulled the baby close to her.

"Shhh, it's okay. He cries a lot. Must be the colic," she said, rocking Daniel until he stopped crying.

Charley could find no words for what he'd witnessed. He mumbled a goodbye and watched Stella leave the park with Daniel in his stroller. Once again, he said nothing. But this time began a precedent. It would be the first of many times he did nothing.

Over the years, Charley saw Stella sporadically. Their affair had long ended but he continued to see her, often with Daniel, either grabbing coffee or meeting in the park. He saw a decline in the woman's mental heath each time he met her and he knew she was not seeing a doctor. Signs of physical abuse were sometimes evident on both Stella and Daniel, but the hollowness of Daniel's eyes seared his soul.

The last time Charley saw Stella alive, he hugged her and wished her well, adding that he would always be there for her.

"A real man would be more than that," she quipped and walked away. He wondered if there was a double meaning behind her words.

It wasn't long after that he heard she'd committed suicide. Her final desperate action sent Charley into despair. He wallowed in self-pity and regret until her funeral. The sight of Daniel leaving the service jolted him out of his selfishness and into making a decision that should have been made years before.

He grabbed his cell phone and made that telephone call to New Mexico. Frank Carpenter had been a childhood friend of his through high school. While Charley's family moved away after graduation, he kept in touch with Frank over the years. He knew his friend would take Daniel in and it was a risk Charley needed to take, for Daniel's sake, and for Stella's.

So now, Charley faced the need to be brave once again. He didn't know just how much to reveal to Daniel when he saw him, choosing not to think of that until he needed to. But he couldn't allow Carl to surprise a son he never wanted and never bothered to look for once he was gone. Charley didn't care how close the man was to death, he was still rotten to the core.

Charley's car inched on, the rain still coming down hard. He realized no one else was on the road at that point. He suddenly panicked, thinking he'd been daydreaming enough to miss the exit to the airport. He didn't know where he was on the road. Damn it, how stupid of him. With weather like this, his full attention should've been on driving, not his past.

He didn't see any signs or road markers, but visibility was so poor he probably couldn't make them out if he had. Reaching down, he turned on the radio, hoping to hear some weather report. There was nothing but static.

Cursing again, he fooled with the dial, trying to find a station, and he didn't see the accident in time to react. Brake lights appeared suddenly and haphazardly, filling the width of his windshield and overcoming him. Charley slammed on his brakes and jerked the steering wheel to the right, causing the car to skid out of control. It finally came to a stop upside down, against a stalled minivan.

Charley was ejected from his car, a faulty seatbelt to blame that he'd never bothered to fix. How ironic, he thought, as his life passed before him. When he'd finally decided to do what was right, he would never get the chance. Death took him quickly.

CHAPTER TWENTY-ONE

"You mean he's on his way?" Sarah asked.

"That's what his message implied," Frank said, setting down his phone.

"I hope it doesn't have anything to do with what you've suspected," Sarah worried.

"We need to brace ourselves for anything," he replied, trying to soothe her thoughts. "It was a pretty bad connection, so I didn't get all of his message. Maybe we're making something out of nothing."

"For someone to call and say they're flying clear across the country and they're on the way, it's probably more than nothing, Frank," she said, putting her head in her hands.

"Look, sweetheart, it's not worth worrying about yet," he began, "as soon as he gets here, we'll know, but until then we can't do anything about it."

"I know that, but we've been through so much already. Maybe I'm on edge, but having a gun pointed at your head will do that to you," she said, referring to the encounter with James Tate.

Frank took his wife into his arms and held her there. Having James in their house and holding Sarah hostage had taken a toll on everyone, including Frank. He blamed himself for allowing it to happen, thinking if he'd only gone to the house before searching the fields, he would've prevented James from getting anywhere near Sarah. He would've probably killed the kid, too, if Joe hadn't intervened. But the worst of it fell on his wife. He had to remember that.

James Tate had been arrested and was sitting in jail. Ed refused to see his son or pay for an attorney. Frank had heard Ed Tate wouldn't see anyone, not even the staff he hired at his ranch. They showed up everyday, did what was expected of them, and left, never encountering their employer. Frank wondered how much of the reclusiveness had to do with disappointment in his son, and how much might be due to being wrong about them. It was never easy to admit mistakes, but when something burned your insides with deep-seeded hatred, the errors were even harder to concede.

"How about we go out to dinner tonight?" Frank asked Sarah, suddenly.

"But what if Charley gets here?" she asked.

"I doubt he will that soon, but if he does, he can wait. It'll take our minds off things," he suggested.

"Sounds good, Frank Carpenter," she said.

"Well, all righty, then, Sarah Carpenter. Where do you think you want to go?" he asked.

"What about that Italian bistro on the square?" she asked.

"I guess that means I need to gussy up a bit. Wouldn't want a smelly old cowboy in a fancy Italian bistro," he smiled.

Sarah smiled at him, kissing his cheek. It was what Frank wanted, something to take her mind from whatever was about to hit within the next twenty-four hours.

———

The devil was on his way. It had been his first time on an airplane and he didn't like it. Nausea overtook him too much as it was when his feet were on the ground, so flying hadn't made things easier for him. His weak and puny body didn't work like it used to and he knew his time was limited. He'd rot in hell for the things he had done in his lifetime, but he didn't care. He had one last thing to do before death took him and flying to New Mexico would help him accomplish it.

He glanced at the man sitting next to him in the car. The private investigator that broke the news of his son's whereabouts drove the rental car in silence. Why in the world, the devil wondered, had anyone wanted to find him, much less pay his fare to come out west, was beyond him. But the PI did, or who ever he was working for paid it, and the devil wasn't about to turn down a free trip, even though he'd spent most of the flight in the bathroom being sick.

They had just left the Albuquerque airport and were on their way, to where the devil had no clue, but he guessed he'd be seeing that spawn of his soon enough. God, he needed a drink. His throat was dry and he began to sweat. Shaking would start soon enough, something the devil had endured for so long he knew the routine of his out-of-control body. Then he'd get sick again. He didn't know if that was the booze or the cancer, but he rarely ate anything and wondered how there'd be anything left to get sick over.

He marveled at the brightness of the sun and the blue sky. Nothing like this back home, he thought. If he'd been an outdoorsman, he would like what he was seeing, but all it did was hurt his eyes, give him a headache and make him want a drink that much more.

Glancing at his gnarled fingers, he wondered what happened to his once strong body. Sure, he'd abused the bottle but no one ever told him it would turn out like this. He was shriveled and stooped, with a yellow pallor that screamed he was dying. Most of his hair was gone and he looked thirty years older than he was. Hell, he'd resorted to relying on a cane to walk. The devil shuddered to think what was next before he took his last breath.

He thought back over his life. Being sober did that to him and he hated it. He'd much rather be drunk and not have to think or remember. His thoughts drifted back to when he first met Stella. He'd been drunk, of course, but she weaved her magic on him and he was hooked. Jealous rages followed them until she died and then he didn't know what to do. The kid up and left and he suspected Charley had something to do with it. Good, old Charley. He was the one thorn that just kept on sticking. The son-of-a-bitch.

If anything good would come out of this trip he was taking, it would be that he could make Charley pay for what he did. The devil was ready to make every last one of them miserable in his last moments, the kid and the family that took him in. It was the only thing that gave him any amount of pleasure. He didn't want to know that the brat was happy. The devil wanted to spit in their faces and watch them squirm when they laid eyes on him. That thought eased his stomach a bit and he leaned back against the seat, closing his eyes and smiling to himself.

CHAPTER TWENTY-TWO

The day was beautiful, as most others, Frank thought, but he could feel fall was just around the corner. Colors would start changing soon and winter would be upon them again in no time. How fast time passed.

Frank and Sarah had made Daniel aware of what was to come that day. They told him Charley would be visiting, so all three of them were sticking close to the house that morning, doing menial tasks that had been put off too long.

"I guess it's been awhile since I puttered around the garden, Sarah," Frank said, watching her deadhead some of the plants.

"Puttered?" Daniel asked, grinning.

"Yeah, puttered. What's so funny?" Frank asked.

"That's just a funny word coming from you," Daniel replied.

"Why? You saying I can't putter?" he asked.

"You go full-barrel, Frank. Puttering is not in your nature," Sarah said, smiling.

"Well, I guess that's why you're better in the garden than I am," Frank sighed.

"You could clean out the gutters or wash some windows, hint, hint," Sarah replied, laughing.

"Not much puttering needed for those jobs," Daniel said.

"C'mon, I guess we've just been assigned jobs to do," Frank said to Daniel.

They started to walk around the house when the sound of a car coming up the path got their attention. Fully anticipating seeing his old buddy Charley, Frank was surprised to see the sheriff pull up to their house.

"Mornin', Frank," the sheriff said as he got out of his car.

"What can we do for you this morning, sheriff?" Frank asked.

"Well, it seems I'm the bearer of some bad news," he replied.

"How so?" Frank asked. Daniel and Sarah stood at his side.

"There's been an accident. I was supposed to pick up your friend Charley at the airport last night. When he didn't get off the flight, I did some checking," the sheriff said, looking at his boots. "Your buddy was in a bad car accident yesterday, Frank. He didn't make it. I'm sorry."

"But he left us a message yesterday," Frank replied, stunned at the news.

"Apparently a big storm hit the area, with lots of tornados touching down. A big pileup on the interstate as a result and Charley was part of it," said the sheriff.

"I can't believe it," was all Frank could say.

"Well, again, I'm sorry. It seems nothing could've been done to prevent it. Poor visibility and all," the sheriff's voice trailed off.

"Sheriff, since you were picking him up, do you know why Charley was coming out here?" Sarah asked.

"You mean you don't?" he asked.

"Vaguely, yes. Specifically, no," she replied.

"Well, I wasn't picking him up out of the goodness of my heart," began the sheriff, "he and I had been in contact over some issues concerning Daniel. He called me with some concerns and I offered to pick him up."

"What kind of concerns?" Frank asked.

"Daniel, your biological father is on his way here to see you," the sheriff said, looking at Daniel and ignoring Frank.

"How do you know?" Daniel asked. His sudden intake of breath was clear. The color had drained from his face. Frank worried his son would panic and run.

"I've had some interesting conversations over the last few weeks. Let's just say a private investigator can find all kinds of information, some you might not want to know," the sheriff replied, looking directly at Frank and Sarah.

"I think you need to spell it out and stop talking in riddles, sheriff. We have nothing to hide," Frank said.

"Well, okay, then. Ed Tate is out to ruin you, no matter what the cost. His PI dug up some dirt and contacted Daniel's father and me. I wanted to verify what I'd been told, so I found your friend, Charley," the sheriff said. "Charley called me yesterday with the news that Daniel's old man was on his way here. So Charley decided to come as well."

"After all this time, why would either one of them care?" Daniel asked.

"It seems your father—" the sheriff began.

"He's not my father. Frank is," Daniel interrupted.

"Okay, I'm sorry. It seems Carl wants to press charges against Frank and Sarah. As for Charley, I think he had a bit on his conscience he wanted to share," the sheriff explained.

"Well, I'm glad I didn't have to hear it," Daniel mumbled.

"You might have found it interesting," the sheriff hinted.

"No, I don't think so," replied Daniel.

"He did help you get here, didn't he?" the sheriff asked.

"Look, you don't know the whole story," Frank said, getting annoyed with the man.

"I believe I know more than you think I do," the sheriff replied.

"Okay, he helped me get here. I'm thankful for that and I'll always be grateful. And I always said I wanted to repay him for it. But for fifteen years, he didn't help. He knew what was going on. I know he kept in touch with Frank and Sarah about me, but I haven't even seen him in the last three years. I'm sorry that he died, I really am," Daniel said, looking away.

"I know you are, son," the sheriff said, sympathetically.

"Look, I want you to be straight with us. What are we facing legally here?" Frank asked.

The sheriff looked directly at Frank. "In my opinion, nothing. I know the story and the history behind everything. I can't even believe the man has the audacity to come here with any claims. But if Daniel were a minor when all this came to light, there'd be a whole boatload of problems to deal with," he said.

The sound of tires on gravel diverted their attention to the drive up the house. They watched as two vehicles slowly approached, leaving a dust trail behind them, and coming to a stop behind the sheriff's car. One looked to be Ed Tate's truck, while the other was an unrecognizable car.

Ed emerged from his truck, pale and gaunt, the effects of his son's actions obviously the cause of weight loss and the dark circles that tinted the skin underneath his eyes. He had a look of dread on his face, as if he didn't want to be part of what was about to happen, but just wanted to get it over with. He stood by the car with his hands on his hips, waiting for the occupants to appear.

Frank watched as the driver's side door opened and a man got out. He was big and heavy, and carried himself easily around the car to help his passenger out. In Frank's gut, he knew the other person in the car was Daniel's father and he waited as the man slowly made himself visible.

Glancing at Daniel, Frank saw the mask of no emotion on his face. Reaching out, he touched his son's shoulder in reassurance and Daniel nodded, as if indicating everything would be okay. Frank guessed he needed reassuring, too.

Finally in sight for them to see, the withered, frail man stood leaning on his cane, squinting in the bright sunshine. Frank was shocked at the image and thought the man could easily fall, as he seemed unsteady on his feet. Was this really the tyrant of Daniel's nightmares? Unable to walk by himself, the PI helped him move closer to the group watching him.

Finally, Ed was the first to speak. Almost embarrassed, he cleared his throat and looked down at his boots.

"Did some checking up, Frank, as I'm sure the sheriff here has filled you in," he said.

"He has," Frank replied.

"Well, I thought things should be made right," Ed said.

"There are some things that are none of your damn business," Frank retorted.

"You're right. That's why I want to make things good," he replied.

"You got me, Ed. I don't know where you're going with this," Frank said.

"I made a mistake stirring all this up. I realize that now. I should've let sleeping dogs lie," said Ed.

"Little late for that," came the feeble cackle from the man leaning against the cane.

"Maybe. Maybe not," Ed said, "but I have to tell you this man is Daniel's father, and him being here is my doing."

"You remember me, Danny boy?" the devil asked, glinting at Daniel.

"You don't look the same," Daniel replied, nodding.

"Well, you don't either. Grown up, have you?" he asked.

When Daniel didn't respond, the devil grew agitated. "Answer your father when he speaks to you, Danny," he spewed.

"My name is Daniel, not Danny. And you aren't my father," Daniel said calmly.

"Like hell I'm not! Raised you, fed you, put a roof over your good-for-nothing head. Then you up and leave, ungrateful bastard," the devil yelled, sending the man into a coughing fit.

He was doubled over with coughing spasms. All watched, thinking the man was going to die right there. He struggled for breath, the private investigator looking helplessly on, holding him up and unable to do anything more for him. When the fit seemed to subside, Daniel chose his words carefully.

"As I recall, you did nothing but knock me around and make my life a living hell every chance you got. I can't seem to muster up any gratitude for that," he said.

"Why, you think you're something now, don't you, boy? Living here on this land with all the uppity people sure has given you a mouth. Well, let me tell you something. You ain't nothing more than you were the day you left," the devil spewed.

"That's enough," Sarah interrupted.

"So the woman wears the pants in the family," the devil said, leering at Sarah.

"I think you need to leave," Frank said, stepping forward.

"I ain't going nowhere," the devil spat.

"Ed, take this slime and get the hell off my property," Frank fumed, turning to Tate.

"You think I came all this way just to be thrown out like garbage?" the devil asked, wheezing.

"This was a bad idea, one that came to light out of ill will. I'm sorry, Frank," Ed said, turning to Carl, "let's go."

"Not before I see some justice," the man replied.

"You don't deserve any justice," Frank said, towering over the devil's form, "and I know you can see the sheriff standing there. I will ask him to intervene if I need to."

"He can intervene all he wants, but it seems you and your wife were the ones who broke the law. Not me," the devil said.

"We took a young man into our home, one so broken he was afraid of his own shadow. You're to blame for that. We provided stability and a good home for him and, I'm happy so say, he's grown into a well-adjusted adult. We love him as our own, like a son," Frank said.

"Well, he ain't your son," the devil spewed.

"Actually, he is," Frank said, crossing his arms.

The devil peered at Frank, as if he hadn't heard correctly, or that he was trying to comprehend the meaning behind the words. His face was a twisted mass of lines and shadows, a roadmap that led to nowhere but telling in the hard life the man chose to live. Daniel spoke.

"I chose to be adopted. I'm now Daniel Carpenter," he said.

"Are you now?" the devil asked, finding his voice. He showed a nearly toothless grin, with the remaining teeth yellowed and rotting.

"We assumed you might have known," Frank said.

"The only thing I knew was what this kindly gentleman shared with me. That Danny boy was alive and kicking in New Mexico, and that you had been harboring a runaway for three years," the devil said, pointing a finger at Frank.

"As I said a minute ago. We were happy to provide a home for him. A real home," Frank said with emphasis.

"Seems to me the whole lot of you stink. You, your wife and that meddling Charley. Always around, he was, making my damn life miserable," the devil said.

"I think you had enough misery to dole out yourself," Frank added.

"Why don't you shut the hell up? Wonder where old Charley boy is. I know he was trying to find me yesterday morning. Gave him the slip," the devil said, smiling.

No one said anything. Then the sheriff stepped forward and introduced himself. "I'm afraid Charley died in a car accident yesterday. You all had some bad weather hit your area," he said.

"Charley, dead? Well, I'll be damned," the devil mumbled, a little dumbfounded. The news stunned the man into silence. His reaction indicated he might have been a little more bothered by the announcement than he would ever admit.

"I guess you got lucky and beat the storm," the sheriff said.

"Yeah, some luck," the devil said, still a little distracted.

"Well, I suggest you follow Frank's advice and leave. Get on the next plane back home. Put all this behind you," said the sheriff.

"So tell me. How does one's own son get adopted right out from under you?" the devil asked.

"The Carpenters applied to legally adopt Daniel once he turned eighteen. As an adult, Daniel had the choice," replied the sheriff.

"And no one bothered to tell me?" he asked.

"It's not required. Sometimes the birth parents are notified, but not always," the sheriff said.

"And I take it no charges will be filed for what they did for three years?" the devil asked, pointing at Frank and Sarah.

"What the Carpenters did for three years was protect Daniel from you. If I were you, I'd let it drop and go home. You don't want me dredging up charges against you, but I will if I have to," the sheriff threatened.

"You don't have nothin' on me," the devil bluffed.

"I know what you've done and it would take nothing to prove it. You'll spend the rest of your miserable life, what little's left of it, in a jail cell," the sheriff said, stepping closer to Carl.

Ed Tate stepped forward and motioned the private investigator. "Let's go," he said.

The investigator took Carl's arm, but the devil wasn't ready to budge yet. Looking at Daniel, he said, "You're the spittin' image of Stella, you know that? Ain't no doubt you're her son."

Then he allowed himself to be directed to the car and helped inside. The investigator closed the door and briefly spoke with Ed. Tate turned and glanced at Frank, nodding while getting in his own truck. The two vehicles left with Ed following the car carrying the devil right out of Daniel's life. Frank hoped for good.

"Thank you," Frank said to the sheriff.

"You're welcome. But I really should be thanking the two of you," he replied, nodding at Frank and Sarah.

"Why is that?" Sarah asked.

"I know what kids mean to both of you. And you did a good thing here. Ed Tate ought to be ashamed of himself, stirring things up like he did," the sheriff said.

"For some reason, I think he was," Frank offered.

"You're probably right. I think his own son's action's caused him to eat a slice or two of humble pie," said the sheriff.

"What about Charley?" Frank asked suddenly, changing the subject.

"What about him? He'd never been married and his only surviving kin is his mother. She's in a nursing home, not doing too well," he said.

"I guess what I'm asking is there anything he wanted us to know, or that we need to know?" Frank asked.

"Maybe someday Daniel might want to know what turned out to be the man's deathbed confessions. But if not, I'd just let bygones be bygones," the sheriff suggested.

"I don't really want to know," Daniel said, shaking his head.

"Well then, my job is done here. Glad I didn't have to arrest anybody. I hate it when that happens," he grinned.

They watched the sheriff drive away and it seemed like the ending to a bad dream. Everything they had been worrying about all summer was over and resolved. Ed and James Tate were no longer threats. Daniel's father wasn't the hidden beast anymore, ready to strike at a moment's notice when they least expected it. Daniel was now Frank and Sarah's legal son and no one could change that fact. They breathed a sigh of relief and the wind of change was in their favor.

CHAPTER TWENTY-THREE

Misfit was running hard. Daniel's sweat mixed with that of the horse as they rode together across the land. The animal had reacted well to Daniel's training and seemed to need the challenge of work and vigorous exercise. He was smart and Daniel appreciated the horse's personality, but he sometimes regressed, taking on the way of the wild he'd been born to.

Misfit was prone to act up, his high spirits often overshadowing the training he'd been through, but Daniel knew it would pass. He was patient, working the horse through a small and slow obstacle course of barrels and cones until his need to disobey subsided. The animal finally learned he had to listen and Daniel had been able to ride him a number of times around the property. And he flew like the wind. He was the fastest horse Daniel had ever ridden and it was easy to feel the spirit of the animal as they glided across the land. It made Daniel feel free, a sensation intensified by the results of the last couple of days.

The devil was gone and all thoughts of him diminished from Daniel's mind. His history with the man and the memories were still there, fresh and hovering, never to be lessened because of the absence. He found there were some things, however, from his past he simply couldn't remember. His counselor said that was his defense mechanism working to protect himself. Perhaps someday those memories would come to the surface but probably not. The nightmares, however, of horror and fear were gone but he guessed they'd rise again occasionally over his lifetime. He'd survive with the reassurance the man could never harm him or anyone he cared about ever again.

It was surprising seeing the man he'd known as his father after three years' time. Physically, he was nothing like the person he remembered, and he certainly didn't resemble the figure in Daniel's nightmares. The devil was shriveled and frail, his body wrecked from cancer and years of rough living. He'd hardly been able to stand on his own. Yet, his tongue was still sharp and his mind full of cruel thoughts he didn't mind sharing with anyone who would listen. Daniel guessed he didn't have much longer to live. For the life of him, he tried to muster some sort of sympathy for the man but couldn't.

He and Misfit approached one of the streams and he decided to let the horse rest and get water. His eyes drank in the scenery as much as Misfit was drinking water. He still couldn't believe he'd be part of this beautiful land for as long as he wanted. The adoption and name change had been finalized and he had never felt so happy. Frank and Sarah had done a generous thing and he vowed to never let them down and to be there for them whenever they needed him.

They'd discussed with him the possibility of taking in the little girl who needed a home. Of course he was supportive of any decision they made. He thought they were both a little nervous about the situation, but interestingly, Frank seemed a bit more excited about it than Sarah. For several days, Frank brought a stuffed animal or little doll home whenever he went out, until Sarah asked him to stop, indicating he'd spoil the child before she ever stepped foot in the house. Daniel smiled. Frank's face was full of anticipation for a little girl. Sarah's was apprehensive. He guessed years of losing children would do that, but he knew Sarah would love the child with all her being. And Daniel couldn't wait to meet her.

His thoughts turned to Maria. She would be leaving for school very soon. She had promised him that she would always come back. He promised her he would always wait. He'd decided to take classes at the community college for a while, starting in the fall. If all that went well, maybe he would follow Maria in a couple of years, but for now he wanted to stay home and help with the ranch and sanctuary.

Home. A word he didn't even understand the meaning of three years ago, but one that the Carpenters had shown the significance of through their kindness and love. He felt the word now and he knew he was home. He wasn't sure if he could ever leave.

Misfit stirred, getting Daniel's attention. The horse nuzzled his neck then lowered his head, sniffing the pocket on Daniel's shirt.

"Sorry, buddy. Nothing for you until we get back," Daniel said, rubbing the horse's neck.

Misfit blew and nodded his head, as if he understood. Daniel laughed. "You really are too smart, you know it? And just why do you think you deserve a treat anyway?"

He got on the horse again and they made their way home, this time at a more leisurely pace. There was that word again. Home. A place you were always going to go.

———

Merrill and Sandra waited for Maria. Merrill fidgeted nervously, alternating between sitting, standing and pacing. He was anxious to get this over with and the sooner Maria got there, the better he would be. He had decided to introduce Sandra and their relationship to his daughter. It was the best decision he hoped.

"Pacing won't make her get here any quicker," Sandra said. She sat calmly, flipping through the pages of a magazine. She didn't fool Merrill. She'd stayed longer on one page than any of the others and it was obvious to him that she was nervous, too.

"I know," he said, sitting down next to her. "This is just so important to me and for us. I want Maria to accept you."

"If what I've heard about Maria is true, she will," Sandra said, soothingly, taking his hand in hers. They sat together like that on the sofa in Merrill's living room. At first, he thought he would take both of them out to dinner somewhere nice and then he and Sandra could explain things then. But the more he thought about it, it didn't seem like such a good idea to break the news to her in a public place. While Merrill was certain Maria would welcome Sandra into his life, he thought it best to play it safe and tell her in the privacy of their home. If all went well, then he planned to take them out to eat afterwards to celebrate.

The sound of the car driving up, then of a door shutting alerted them to her arrival. They waited tensely, as if an unknown force was about to determine their fate. Merrill knew Maria's approval or disapproval wouldn't change the way he and Sandra felt about each other. They weren't going to end their relationship. He just wanted his daughter to be part of his life. All of it with no secrets. It was a fresh start with a new beginning and he wanted to do it before Maria left for school.

"Hi, Papa," Maria said, as she came through the door, glancing at him and then Sandra.

"Hi, little girl," he replied, standing up. "I'd like to introduce you to someone."

Then Merrill began talking. He felt his mouth moving faster than his brain could think, but it felt good. It was like a rush of rusty, stale air being expelled while he gulped for fresh, clean newness, giving him energy and hope for new life. When he stopped talking, he felt lighter for some reason, as if by talking he'd unleashed a burden of weight from his shoulders. He took Sandra's hand and they stood together in front of his daughter, waiting for a response.

Maria smiled softly at her father. "Papa, you didn't have to explain anything to me," she began, "I already guessed."

"What? How?" Merrill asked, confused.

"I could tell when I worked at the Turnout. Most of the time, you're serious and somber, but I'd see a change at times when you'd get on the phone. Your face relaxed and you smiled and joked. I knew you had to be talking to someone special," she replied, glancing at Sandra and smiling.

"I don't know what to say," Merrill mumbled.

"You don't have to say anything, Merrill. It's out in the open now, and I sense you have Maria's approval to be happy," Sandra said.

Maria nodded and went to her father, hugging him. She kissed his cheek and then gave Sandra a welcoming embrace. Seeing his child do this let Merrill know it really was going to be okay.

CHAPTER TWENTY-FOUR

Frank was so excited he could hardly contain himself. He'd risen earlier than normal because he could no longer sleep. Showering, he got ready for their big day, trying not to awaken Sarah. He watched his wife as he buttoned his shirt, thinking how peaceful and beautiful she looked. Her hair fanned across the pillow and the light from their bathroom cast her face in softness. The gentle rise and fall of her shoulders indicated she was in a deep sleep. How she'd been able to get a minute's rest was beyond him, but he also knew she'd tossed and turned some the night before. Sarah was worried more than he was about the step they were taking. At least she'd been able to get to sleep eventually.

There was something about this child coming into their home that caused him to act plain silly. He knew he was doing it, and he knew everyone else noticed it, but for the life of him he couldn't help it. He'd seen the way Daniel's face lit up with amusement whenever a world of goofiness overcame him. Bill and Inez had just ignored him, probably not knowing how to react to his antics. Sarah would stare at him, then shake her head with an, "oh, Frank," trying hard to hide a smile that he always caught.

But they were going to parent a little girl, and as much as it elated him, it also scared him. He wasn't bothered by the worry that plagued Sarah, rather he was afraid of doing something wrong. Daniel's demons came into their home with him and they had to be parents to him in a different manner. He'd been shaped and molded a certain way and they had to undo a lot of the emotional turmoil that plagued him. And they related to him on an adult level. But this was a child, with a fairly clean slate, and it was up to them to bring her up the right way. He just didn't want to make any mistakes.

He still couldn't believe their good fortune after all this time. They had a son come into their lives and they couldn't ask for a better person to call their own. Daniel was decent, caring, kind and compassionate. He listened with an open ear and was willing to lend a hand at a moment's notice. And now, the possibility of adopting a daughter completed him for some reason. Yes, she was young, and she would have some physical limitations, but none of that mattered. His heart felt full of love that morning for everyone in his life.

Sarah stirred, stretching her arms above her head. "Hey, sleepy head," he said, watching her wake up. "You going to sleep all day?"

"No, just had trouble getting to sleep, that's all," she replied, yawning. "You're already dressed!"

"I woke up early and couldn't get back to sleep," he said, "so, I thought I'd get up and at 'em."

"You're excited to meet her, aren't you?" Sarah asked, reaching for his hand.

"Very," Frank replied, sitting on the bed beside her. "Aren't you?"

"I am. I'm so scared, Frank," she told him.

"I know you are," he said, "but you and I have been through a lot together. Whatever this brings, I'll always be there for you, darlin'."

"What if there are problems?" she asked.

"What if there aren't?" he asked in response.

"Did anyone ever tell you that you're not supposed to answer a question with a question?" she asked, teasing him.

"Is that what you're telling me now?" he asked, grinning.

"You're impossible," she replied, stifling a yawn.

"And that's why you love me, I know it," he said. "Why don't you get in the shower? I'll make us some breakfast."

"Oh, all right," she began, "Frank, I love you." Sarah stared at her husband with hopefulness and fear written on her face. Frank always wanted to protect her when she looked that way.

"I love you, too, Sarah," he replied, his eyes bright. He kissed her hand and pulled her close. Her warm frame fit comfortably into the folds of his arms. She rested her head against his shoulder and seemed to draw strength from him. It was the same for him. Frank didn't know what he'd do if something ever happened to Sarah. She was his reason for going on everyday. He couldn't imagine living without her.

He busied himself in the kitchen while she got ready. Coffee made, Frank poured a cup and stood drinking it while he stared out of the kitchen window. He thought back to when James Tate got in the house. They'd since started locking doors during the day and keeping gates locked at all times. All of that probably wasn't necessary but he didn't dare take any more chances. He was investigating a better security system with a phone at the gates to announce deliveries and guests. It was something that should've been done long ago, but he'd never gotten around to it, thinking stupidly that they would never be victims of a crime, even when they knew the Tates were threatening them.

"Morning. Looks like you beat me to it," Daniel said, coming into the room.

"Morning to you. And what did I do?" Frank asked, sipping his coffee.

"Got to the coffee first, and I was going to surprise you two with breakfast," he said, nodding at the griddle Frank had set on the burners.

"Well, help yourself to coffee and you can help me cook, too," Frank replied.

"So, I take it you're a little excited for today," Daniel said, smiling behind his coffee mug.

"You know I am and I don't care if I've been acting like the village idiot," Frank smirked.

"It's all okay," Daniel laughed.

"Daniel," Frank began, "you know that bringing another child into our home doesn't change the way Sarah and I feel about you being our son."

"I know. You don't have to explain anything," he replied.

"Yes, I do. Nothing will change, I want you to know that. We're just adding another person," Frank said.

"I think it'll be cool to have a little sister. I've never had one," he said, taking a carton of eggs from the refrigerator.

"Well, we hope it works out all right. We've been down this road many times before, only to be disappointed. Sarah's real worried about it," Frank said.

"I could tell. I'll do all I can to help," Daniel reassured him.

"I know you will," Frank nodded.

"You'll be disappointed, too, right? If it doesn't work out," Daniel asked.

"I suppose I will," Frank replied.

"What usually happens? I mean when it doesn't work out?" he asked.

"We've dealt with kids who don't want to be here to parents who got cold feet and changed their minds," Frank said. "The hardest ones were the parents who came for the kids. The older ones who didn't want to live with us for whatever reason, we knew it wouldn't work out, so there was no surprise there. But the children you got attached to that were taken away by their biological parents, those were tough. You always felt like you'd been sucker punched."

"I can't imagine a kid not wanting to live here," Daniel replied.

"A few didn't. Of those, most didn't want to follow rules, do chores and be responsible and respectful. Actually had one boy steal some money from us," Frank said.

"What did you do?" asked Daniel.

"He had to go. He'd been trouble from the moment he stepped in the house. Naively, we just thought we could work with him and help him. Didn't work out that way," said Frank.

"Some people don't want to be helped," Daniel mused

"Some people don't have it in them to allow help. They think it's being weak, I guess," Frank replied.

"Maybe that's why Carl ended up the way he was," mumbled Daniel, lost in thought. It was the first time Frank had heard Daniel call his biological father by his given name, or even reference the man as a human being.

"Listen, I don't know Carl's history. But I know one thing for certain. Nothing justifies the way he treated you. Nothing. You're the polar opposite of that man, Daniel. As long as you remember that and continue to be the good person we know you to be, you'll go far in life," Frank said.

"I know I'm not like him, but I've always been afraid I would be," Daniel replied.

"I can understand why you'd fear that. He wasn't a good role model, that's for sure," offered Frank.

"No, he wasn't. Neither was Stella," Daniel said.

"Well, you recognize it. And you can go to counseling for as long as you need to. Whatever it takes to make you feel whole again, Daniel. That's what Sarah and I want for you," Frank said.

"I know she was sick, Stella that is. But it still didn't give her the right to do the things she did," Daniel said.

"You're right, it didn't. From what I understand, she refused to get any help," Frank offered.

"I don't want to be like her either," Daniel said, his eyes bright. "I worry about that everyday."

"I know you do, Daniel, and I don't think you are. I really don't. Sarah and I are always here for you," Frank said.

Daniel nodded and changed the subject. "What happened to the kid who stole the money? I mean after he left here," he said.

"The social worker knew of another family willing to take him in. The couple was older with two adult sons who helped work with him. They set pretty strict rules for him to follow, he got involved with a youth group at their church and apparently it worked for him. That family was what he needed. Last I heard, he'd joined the military, married and moved to California," Frank explained.

"I'm glad it worked out," Daniel mused.

"Me, too. Most times all it takes is finding the right family," Frank offered, smiling at Daniel. "I'd better get cooking or Sarah will get down here and not let me do it."

"Well, if I had my choice," Daniel grinned.

"Yeah, yeah, I would rather have Sarah's cooking, too. But you gotta admit, I make a mean omelette," Frank said.

"Yes, you do, but that's not the pan to use for omelettes," Daniel teased, nodding at the griddle.

"This old cowboy knows how to cook, don't you worry. I thought I'd make a feast of pancakes, too," Frank grinned, rubbing his hands together.

Sarah joined them shortly, eating her breakfast and adding to the conversation, casually laughing at things Frank or Daniel would say. Frank thought she looked exceptionally beautiful that morning, but he saw the shadows under her eyes from the lack of sleep and worry. He wished he could reassure her this time would be different, but he couldn't guarantee anything.

They were cleaning up the kitchen when the sound of a car coming up the drive got their attention. Frank had asked Bill to unlock the gate earlier that morning, so their guests wouldn't have to wait. The three of them went outside and watched the blue minivan arrive.

Marjorie, the woman who initially told Sarah about the child, got out of the driver's side of the van and walked around to the other side. Saying hello to them, she opened the side door and reached in to unfasten a booster seat. They watched as she gently lifted the little girl out of the van and set her on the ground. Marjorie reached in the van, retrieved the child's stuffed bunny and handed it to her.

Turning to face them, Marjorie took the little girl's hand and walked slowly toward Frank, Sarah and Daniel. Clutching the worn out bunny rabbit under the opposite arm, she held tightly to Marjorie's hand, apprehension showing in her expressive, large eyes. Her slight limp drew their attention to the brace, nearly hidden under her right pant leg. With hair the color of honey that reached just to her shoulders, the little girl looked at them with wonder. Frank could feel his heart melting as he watched Sarah's face soften, the lines of fear giving way to a welcoming smile.

"Good morning, everyone. I'd like you to meet Annie," Marjorie said, introducing each of them to the child.

Annie looked directly at all three of them and answered with, "Good morning," before turning to Daniel. "Are you my uncle?" she asked him in a little high-pitched voice.

Daniel knelt before her and said, "No, but I'd like to be your big brother, if you'd let me."

"I've never had a big brother before!" Annie said, her mouth turning upward into a wide grin.

"Well, I'd like to be your big brother, Annie. Would you like that?" Daniel asked her.

"Yes," she nodded vigorously, her sweet smile turning her face into laughter. The sound was music to Frank's ears. He felt Sarah's hand slip into his.

"And what is my big brother's name?" Annie asked, still laughing.

"My name is Daniel," he replied.

"I like that name," Annie said, seriously.

They showed Marjorie and Annie around inside the house, including the room that would be Annie's bedroom. The little girl seemed impressed with all of the stuffed animals Frank had acquired and placed on the child's bed. Staring at them, she sighed and finally asked, "Can Frumpy sleep with them, too?"

"Who's Frumpy, Annie?" Sarah asked.

Annie held up the one-eyed bunny rabbit she carried under her arm. "This is Frumpy."

"Of course, Frumpy can sleep with them. They can't wait to meet him," Sarah replied, smiling.

Annie regarded Sarah with a serious face. After considering what she had to say, Annie blurted, "Can I call you Mommy?"

Sarah sat on the edge of the bed, facing the child. "I'd like that very much," she replied.

That response made Annie smile once again. Then the child looked at Frank. Staring at him with wide eyes, she slowly brought the stuffed rabbit forward. "Would you like to hold Frumpy?" she asked him.

"Are you sure he'd want me to hold him?" Frank asked, kneeling before her.

"Yes, he would," replied Annie, solemnly, nodding her head.

"Then I would love to hold him," Frank replied, taking the stuffed animal from her.

Reaching up, Annie placed her small hands on either side of Frank's face, taking him by surprise. "I think I'd like to call you Daddy," she said simply before removing her hands. The action and her words made it hard for him to reply right away. Finally he was able to respond with, "I'd like that, Annie." And she seemed content with letting him hold Frumpy.

After discussing particulars with Marjorie, they walked back outside to unload Annie's few belongings and luggage from the minivan. As they said their goodbyes to Marjorie, one of the horses neighed, bringing Annie's attention toward the sound.

"Is that a pony?" she squealed, her eyes wide, as she looked toward the horses in the nearest paddock. She apparently hadn't noticed them when she first arrived.

"Those are horses, Annie," replied Daniel. "Would you like to see them?"

"Oh, yes, please!" she replied, clapping her hands together.

"Hey, Annie, would you like to ride on Daniel's back to see the horses?" Sarah asked her, noting the child's brace and special shoe. They'd have to see about getting her some boots made to be outdoors with the horses.

Annie nodded in response, and Daniel bent down allowing the child to climb onto his back. Frank and Sarah followed them to the paddock, while the horses eagerly greeted them at the gate, curious about the newcomer. They nickered and nuzzled, heads up and each vying for attention. Daniel and Frank explained where to touch the animals, as Annie gently reached in to stroke the neck of the nearest gelding. The horse softly blew through its nose, the sound making Annie jump back, and causing her to laugh out loud. The child's laugh was foreign to the horses, their ears pricked up and swiveled in the direction of the sound. They were as interested in her and she in them.

"Annie, if you think this is something, maybe someday you can ride one of them," Frank suggested, unable to wipe the silly grin from his face but didn't care who saw it.

"Really?" she gasped. "I would like that," she nodded.

"It looks like she's already getting a ride," Bill said, coming from the barn. He pointed to Annie on Daniel's back. Joe walked out, a few steps behind him.

"You have a limp, too," Annie said to Joe solemnly, looking at his legs.

Her comment surprised Joe, as no one really discussed his limp so openly. Then seeing part of the brace on her leg, his face relaxed and he gave Annie a smile. "Yes, I do, but I don't have the cool brace on my leg though," he replied.

"You think it's cool?" she asked, glancing around at her leg. "All the other kids make fun of it."

"I think it's very cool," Joe said, his heart going out to her, as he understood what she said more than she could possibly know.

"Will you be my uncle?" Annie asked Joe.

"I'll be your uncle if you'd like," Joe replied, giggling at the child.

"Okay. What's your name?" she asked.

"You can call me Uncle Joe," he replied, glancing at Daniel and remembering how they first met. Similar words he recalled.

"Why don't we ask Uncle Joe to go with us to find Bob," Daniel suggested.

"Who's Bob? Can he be an uncle, too?" Annie asked.

"Bob is the greatest dog in the world. I'm sure he won't mind being your uncle, too," Daniel replied.

"A dog?" Annie asked, breathlessly.

"Yep, a dog," Joe replied. "Oh, and nice bunny rabbit, Mr. C," he nodded to Frank.

Frank realized he was still holding Frumpy and all he could do was nod at Joe, who was already turning toward Daniel and Annie.

The three of them moved to find Bob when Daniel said, "Boy, you're heavy, Annie."

"I'm not heavy," she squealed in reply, laughing out loud.

When they were out of sight, Bill turned to Sarah and Frank. "Congratulations. She's adorable," he said, heading back toward the barn.

"Yes, she is adorable," Sarah replied to her husband. "And she already has all the men wrapped around her tiny little fingers."

"Nah, we're not that whipped, are we?" Frank teased.

"Yes, you are. You're standing out here holding a stuffed bunny rabbit, Frank. I bet old Bob will be next. That dog will be following her around everywhere," Sarah replied, smiling at her husband.

"You mind?" Frank asked, skeptically.

"I love it," she replied, putting her arms around his waist. "Between you, Daniel and Joe, she'll probably never be allowed to date anyone because none of you will think any poor boy will be good enough."

"Well, they won't," he grinned, " and I do have a lot of shotguns if necessary."

"I'm glad she'll be looked after," Sarah replied. "She might not appreciate it when the time comes, but I will."

Sarah giggled into her husband's neck. She knew they were doing the right thing and it felt good.

CHAPTER TWENTY-FIVE

Daniel and Maria found their way back to the old kiva. They'd spent much of the day together, sharing a picnic lunch by the stream after horseback riding. She would be leaving Monday to go back to her mom's and then on to college. They'd have the weekend and that would be it for a while. Daniel wasn't sure how he'd feel once she was gone. He had told her he would be fine but a lonely dread was gnawing in the pit of his stomach.

"Annie sure is excited about your birthday party tomorrow," Maria said.

"I think party-planner is her future career," Daniel laughed.

"Well, she's made enough signs and she told me she was helping Sarah make cupcakes," said Maria.

"Yeah, you'd think she was fourteen and not four. She's a bundle of energy," Daniel replied.

"She's a sweetheart, that's for sure, and she seems very happy," Maria offered.

"She is. And she's made all of us happy, too," replied Daniel.

"Why does she call Joe, 'Uncle Joe'?" she asked.

"Apparently, Annie got teased some about her brace. You know, kids can be pretty mean to each other. Anyway, one day at her preschool, I guess she was told she didn't have a family or uncles because no one loved her. Pretty cruel to say, and for that reason, I guess, it stuck in her head," Daniel explained.

"Yes, that's pretty mean. Poor Annie. But she has you and the Carpenters now," Maria said, touching his arm.

"And even Uncle Joe," Daniel joked, smiling.

"Yes, even Uncle Joe, who I must say is smitten with her," Maria laughed.

"That's easy to be when you're around the little squirt," Daniel said, reaching for her and pulling her close. He kissed her there by the old kiva, the place he took her to first and shared his experience of Espíritu and his band of horses. She never thought him strange or odd because of his background, or his nightmares or what he'd endured for the first fifteen years of his life. Maria didn't judge or question or treat him as if something was wrong with him, even though he doubted himself all of the time. Maria accepted him as her equal. God, he was going to miss her.

They held hands and began to walk, past the kiva and along sanctuary land. The scent of sage was strong and Daniel thought it would always remind him of this time, when Maria was about to leave him. He shouldn't think of it that way because they weren't breaking up, but for someone in love it was hard to imagine being without the person who'd stolen your heart.

"See that cottonwood over there?" Daniel asked. He pointed to the knarly looking tree, its shape bent and twisted by time and the elements.

"Yes, it reminds me of something old, kind of like our tribal ancestors looking over us in a way," Maria suggested.

"Something that's withstood the test of time," he murmured. "I used to come here a lot when I first moved here. The old kiva was a place I'd go to help me clear my head but I was always looking for something to give me hope. And I'd always come back to this tree. It amazed me how nothing could break it. Snowstorms, wind, lightning. Nothing ever brought it down. It would bend, but never break. I hoped I would be like that. A survivor. That old tree just gave me faith, I guess," he explained.

"It gave you hope for the future," Maria said.

"I suppose it did. Symbolic, isn't it?" he asked. "I just want to be as tough as that old tree."

"It's your Esperanza, your hope," she suggested.

"I like that," he said. "Come with me." He led her to the base of the cottonwood, its trunk misshapen and rough. The leaves on the branches gently fluttered with the mild breeze, as if speaking to him to stand tall.

The tree at his back, Daniel faced Maria and, with all the bravery he could muster, he had to tell her how he felt. If he didn't, he could regret it for the rest of his life. "Maria," he began, "I don't know how to say this." He looked down at the ground, as if the words were there to find.

"Just say it," she said, quietly. He almost didn't hear her.

"My heart is pounding in my chest, I'm so nervous," he whispered.

"You don't have to be nervous around me," she said.

"Do you believe in love? Love between two people as young as us?" he asked.

Maria nodded, her eyes never leaving Daniel's face. He thought if he stared into her eyes long enough, he'd be able to see clear to her soul. That's how open and clear and giving they were to him in that moment. He wanted honesty between the two of them and he had to tell her how he felt.

"The way the sun rises in the morning and gives light to everything it touches, the way it sets in the evening and gives peace. The way rain falls from the sky and blesses everything that drinks it in. All these things you do for me, Maria," he said. "I'm going to do my best to make it through weeks without seeing you, but it's going to be so hard. All because I love you so much it hurts."

He couldn't look at her now. Those words had been so difficult for him to say and they should have been easy. He'd never been shown love until he moved in with Frank and Sarah, so the capacity for feeling and expressing it were difficult. He knew he could give love but he'd never felt worthy of receiving it. Daniel thought he would understand if Maria couldn't love him in return.

But she put her hand under his chin and raised his face so his eyes would meet hers. And even if she hadn't said what her true feelings were, Daniel saw what she felt, reflected openly in her stare for him to take and drink. He put his arms around her and closed his eyes, wanting to take in the warmth and scent of her to sustain him through the coming weeks.

"Daniel, this has been on my mind so long. I'm dreading going away. I don't want to leave. I want to stay here and be with you. I love you, too, so much," she told him.

"Maria, you have to go," he said. He didn't want her to but knew it was the best thing for her.

"I don't have to. I can stay here and take classes with you. We can be together, Daniel," she said, trying to get him to understand.

"I would like nothing more than for you to stay. But we both know the best thing for you and for our future is for you to go away. We'll talk and text everyday and see each other on weekends when we can. Then Christmas will be here and I'll get to see you for even longer," he urged.

"But I'm going to be miserable and the time will drag by," she said.

"It'll go faster than you think. I promise. Besides, Merrill would have my head if you didn't go," he said, smiling at her.

"We could talk to him. He'd understand eventually," she urged.

"He might come around, Maria, but he'd resent me and I don't want that. It's important that he respect me and trust I'll do right by you," he replied.

"He likes you, Daniel. That wouldn't change if I decided to stay here," she said.

"It might. If it were me, I can't say I'd feel any different. Look at me," he said, putting his hands on her shoulders, "I know it's just a promise right now, but I want to promise you forever. That means some day I want to marry you and have a family with you. I don't know when it'll be but that's my promise, if you'll have me. And it's important Merrill and your mom approve because they're important to you," he stressed.

Maria nodded, looking at him. "Did you just propose?" she asked.

"I guess I did," he replied, grinning.

"Okay," she said, smiling.

"Did you just accept?" he asked.

"I guess I did," she teased. "I accept your promise and give you mine in return."

"And that's enough for now. School is important, Maria. Tell me you're going as you'd planned," he urged. He wanted so badly to throw it all in the wind and agree with her. But encouraging it was selfish and could lead to a whole lot of resentment later on their lives. They had to be patient.

"I will," she nodded, "but it isn't going to be easy."

"You're right, it won't. But it will be worth it," he stressed, pulling her close once again.

They made their promise under the worn cottonwood, the tree that stood tall, its battle scars visible. The symbol of hope that had encouraged Daniel he too could be strong and weather the storms life tossed at him seemed to wrap its branches around them in assurance. Daniel's hope, his Esperanza as Maria suggested, silently witnessed their pledge, its leaves swaying in approval.

EPILOGUE

Daniel Carpenter breathed deeply, the windows down on his pickup truck, the late spring air filled his lungs and rejuvenated him. It was good to be home. He couldn't believe how much he'd missed the ranch and the horses, not to mention Frank, Sarah and Annie. His family. It amazed and filled him with wonder every time he said those words and it probably always would. But he now understood what it meant to have one.

He drove up to the old kiva, the spring thaws cleared making the road passable. The kiva stood as it had the first time he'd laid eyes on it, the crumbling remnants a reminder of an ancient Anasazi past.

Daniel unlocked the gate to the sanctuary's land and let himself in. He walked until he found the old cottonwood, still standing proudly. Much had happened in the nearly four years since he and Maria made their promise to each other under that tree.

Both of them were now college graduates. Maria had gone away to school as planned and Daniel had to admit it was tough getting through those first two years with her away. But he'd taken classes locally and kept busy with ranch duties, until it was time to follow her to school two years later.

And the time away from home was difficult even though he was with Maria. The ranch and the horses were in his blood, flowing through his veins and giving him life. It was where he was meant to be and he had no plans to leave again. Maria felt the same, her time with Merrill reawakening her desire to know more about her ancestry.

Daniel smiled when he remembered Annie's reaction to him getting home. Her exuberance was as spirited as ever but had transferred to a lanky eight-year-old body. She was still tiny, but her arms and legs seemed out of proportion to the rest of her form and when she saw Daniel, she threw herself at him, nearly tackling him in the process. Her laughter at what she'd nearly caused rang through the house and made everyone else laugh.

Annie still wore a brace on her foot, but physical therapy was helping her walk better. She was proud to point out that she could walk with less of a limp, but Daniel noticed when she got tired, her limp was still pronounced.

Horses helped her and Sarah's equine therapy program was in full swing. She had a staff of therapists and counselors who participated in classes and sessions she held four days a week in the riding arena. Positive word of mouth had helped the program expand. Daniel had noticed someone familiar at the program. The security guard who once confronted them at the rodeo was now working part-time for Sarah, helping the kids and doing any odd jobs Sarah asked of him. He seemed genuinely happy to have found new employment.

Joe was in college now and Daniel hadn't seen him as much as he would've liked. He looked forward to his friend's summer break when he'd soon be home and they would no doubt be entertained with Annie's giddiness of having her Uncle Joe and brother Daniel home together with her.

Merrill and Sandra married the summer after Maria's freshman year, waiting so she could come home and be part of the ceremony. The wedding celebration was simple and traditional, just like the couple, who were expecting their first child together soon.

If there was ever a man who deserved the happiness and success he was enjoying, it was Frank. Daniel could see the contentment on his face and he knew much of it had to do with the fact Frank and Sarah had officially adopted both him and Annie. There had been no setbacks or complications with Annie's adoption process and Daniel knew it was a relief to both of them.

Frank's joy was reflected with Annie's first Christmas in their home. The man literally donned a Santa suit one evening, surprising all of them, even Sarah. Of course, Annie saw right through it, Daniel remembered, smiling. She wanted to know why her daddy was dressed up like Santa Claus because Santa wouldn't smell like horses. He'd smell like reindeer, she reasoned. None of them could get from her how reindeer were supposed to smell.

The alfalfa hay production was going well, with last year's crop being the least profitable. Hale storms and unusual rain had damaged much of it. They had been able to get through the winter months with careful rationing for the sanctuary horses. Frank feared they'd lose some valuable customers since he just didn't have the quality hay or amount he'd produced in the past, but most assured him they would buy from him again. No one can control Mother Nature, they told him.

Frank and Sarah had also bought Ed Tate's old place. The man came by one day to make amends and apologize for the trouble he and his son had caused them. He said he'd decided to sell his ranch and move to Montana. James Tate was serving time and Ed didn't know if he could ever face his son again. He wanted to sell because the place held too many memories for him. After much negotiating, Frank and Sarah made him an offer and he accepted. They still hadn't done anything with the land, but were thinking of either expanding the sanctuary grounds or moving the therapy program to the Tate property.

Daniel glanced at the cottonwood again. He and Maria had made a promise to each other under that tree. They planned to keep it by making their engagement official, although he suspected Frank and Sarah already knew. Merrill and Sandra probably did, too.

Something moved then and caught Daniel's eye. He looked just past the tree and saw his old friend, Espíritu. The stallion was watching him, his head up and ears forward. As if remembering Daniel was a friend, the horse slowly sauntered toward Daniel, his head lowered and his tail swishing casually, as if he hadn't a care in the world. Then the great stallion's harem appeared behind him, the horses spreading out and grazing, watching for any aggressive movement that might send them running. The slightest flash of dun caused his eyes to catch the newest member of Espíritu's band. A foal that probably wasn't more than a few days old stuck close to its dam, peeking around the horse's legs at Daniel and wondering what it was seeing for the first time. The foal's long legs were awkward for its body, but it looked healthy. Daniel knew it was capable of running if the band felt the need to flee. Looking closer, Daniel could see the same dorsal stripe that the stallion had.

Espíritu stood about five feet from Daniel, close enough to satisfy his curiosity but far enough away to make a run for it if he needed to.

"Well, my friend, I see you have a new addition," he said to the stallion. The horse nickered a bit, as if confirming what Daniel said.

"I can't tell if it's a colt or a filly from this far away, but I think I'll name it Esperanza, if that's okay with you," Daniel said quietly. Espíritu slowly stepped forward, just close enough for the horse to slightly nuzzle Daniel's arm. Then the stallion backed away and trotted toward his herd. The great horse's head was up and he stopped suddenly and turned to look back at Daniel, and he watched as the band decided to move as one.

Daniel thought back to his first encounter with the great stallion. His many trips to the old kiva giving him strength to go on and get past the memories Carl had inflicted on him. He'd been given strength from all of it and hope for the future. Frank and Sarah were part of that, too, and of his healing. Esperanza. His hope.